Deenie

JUDY BLUME

MACMILLAN CHILDREN'S BOOKS
in association with Heinemann

First published in Great Britain 1980 by William Heinemann Ltd
First published 1983 by Pan Books Ltd
Reissued 1998 by Macmillan Children's Books

This edition published 2015 by Macmillan Children's Books
an imprint of Pan Macmillan
20 New Wharf Road, London N1 9RR
Associated companies throughout the world
www.panmacmillan.com

ISBN 978-1-4472-8682-0

3 5 7 9 8 6 4 2

A CIP catalogue record for this book is available from
the British Library.

Printed and bound by CPI Group (UK) Ltd, Croydon, CR0 4YY

Chapter 1

My mother named me Deenie because right before I was born she saw a movie about a beautiful girl named Wilmadeene, who everybody called Deenie for short. Ma says the first time she held me she knew right away that if she named me Deenie I would turn out the same way — beautiful, that is. I was only four hours old then. And it took me almost thirteen years to find out what *really* happened to the Deenie in the movie. She went crazy and wound up on the funny farm. Ma says I should just forget about that part of the story.

The reason I know about it is the movie was on TV last night and I saw it. Even Helen, who is my older sister, who never watches anything on TV, stayed up late to see the original Deenie. It was a great movie. I really liked it, especially the scenes between Deenie and Bud. He was this guy who was madly in love with her. It was all very romantic, even when she went crazy.

There's a boy named Buddy Brader in eighth grade and I think he's kind of nice. So it is possible that there might be a real-life Deenie and Bud some day, right here in Elizabeth, New Jersey.

This morning I wanted to sleep late. Everybody I know sleeps late on Saturdays but I couldn't because me and Ma had an appointment in New York.

My father drove us downtown in plenty of time to catch the nine-thirty bus. Before we got out of the car Ma said, 'Wish us luck, Frank. This could be the big day.'

'Just be yourself, Deenie,' Daddy told me. 'No matter what happens.'

'I'll try,' I said.

Daddy touched my cheek. Then he turned to Ma. 'Do you need any money?' he asked her.

'I've got enough,' she said. 'We're not doing any shopping.'

'Well then . . . have a good time.'

Ma leaned over and kissed him.

The bus stops on the corner by Old Lady Murray's news-stand. Ma bought a magazine and a pack of gum from her. I try not to look at Old Lady Murray because she's so ugly she makes me want to vomit. She has a big bump on her back and she can't stand up straight. You can see the bump right through her clothes. Even in winter, when she wears an old black coat, you can see it. That's a fact. But today it was warm and sunny, just the way it always is in September when you're wishing it would hurry and get cold. And Old Lady Murray was wearing a plain cotton dress. I pretended to be window shopping so I wouldn't have to look her way.

I was happy when the New York bus finally came down the street. 'Hey, Ma . . .' I called. 'Here's the bus.'

As we got on, the bus driver greeted me with, 'Hi, Beautiful!'

Ma gave him a big smile and said, 'Deenie's the beauty, Helen's the brain.'

The bus driver didn't say anything else because what does he know about our family? He was probably sorry he bothered with us in the first place. I hate it when Ma brags about me and Helen. One time Midge and Janet were over and Ma started in about Helen's brain and my face and I almost died! Later, I told her, 'Please don't do that again, Ma. You embarrassed me in front of my friends.' But Ma just laughed and said, 'I was only telling the truth, Deenie.'

Ma took our tickets from the bus driver and sat down in the second row of seats, next to the window. She dusted off the seat next to her with a tissue before she'd let me sit in it. Then she settled back and pretty soon she was dozing off. I looked out the window for a while but the view from the New Jersey Turnpike's not so hot, so I started thinking instead.

My mother wants me to be a model, with my face on all the magazine covers. Ma says I'll make a lot of money and maybe get discovered for the movies too. A teenage model has to make it by

3

the time she's seventeen if she's ever going to make it big. So the next four years will be very important to me. The thing that really scares me is I'm not sure I want to be a model. I would never tell that to Ma, but I've told Daddy. He says I don't have to be unless I want to.

Today is the third time this month that we're going to a modelling agency. The first one Aunt Rae read about in *TV Guide*. It was an ad that said, 'Be a model or just look like one.' When we got to that agency the lady in charge told my mother that I had a lot of potential and wouldn't Ma like to enrol me in a modelling course for only $250? They'd be able to teach me how to walk the right way and everything.

But Ma told the lady, 'My daughter already knows how to walk and with her face we don't need to pay anybody. Shes the one who's going to get paid.'

After that Ma and Aunt Rae found out about some real modelling agencies. The kind that gets you paying jobs. We went to one two Saturdays ago. The lady there told Ma they were very interested in me, except for my posture, which wasn't great. Since then I've been walking around with books on my head. I hope that's helped, so Ma will leave me alone.

The bus stopped at the Port Authority building on Eighth Avenue. We rode the escalator down to the main level and walked outside to the corner where we took the crosstown bus. 'Once you get started modelling we'll be able to afford taxis,' Ma said.

'That'll be nice,' I told her. My feet were already hurting. Ma says I should stop wearing sneakers. They make your feet spread so your regular shoes don't fit right any more.

When we got to the modelling agency there were two girls waiting to be interviewed ahead of me. I sat down next to one of them. She was by herself. I guess she was at least sixteen and very pretty.

She had her portfolio on her lap. My mother carries mine. It's like a loose-leaf notebook filled with photographs of me. Ma hired this guy to take a whole mess of pictures over the summer. In some of them I'm wearing wigs. I think I look kind of funny and much older than I really am.

'Are you a model?' I asked the girl.

'Yes,' she said. 'Are you?'

'I'm just getting started. Is it fun?'

'It's okay,' she said. 'It's a lot harder than most people think. You have to sit under hot lights for hours. Sometimes I get so bored I practically fall asleep.'

'I thought it would be more exciting than that,' I said.

'The money's pretty good,' she told me. 'That's

why I do it. I hope I get this job. It could lead to a commercial.'

The receptionist called, 'Rachel Conrad . . .' and the girl next to me stood up.

'Good luck,' I said.

'Thanks. You too.'

When Rachel came out the receptionist called, 'Linda Levin . . .' and this very tall girl got up and went in.

'We're next, Deenie,' Ma said.

'I have to go to the bathroom,' I whispered.

'Now? You should have thought of that before.'

'I didn't have to go before.'

'Well, hurry up.'

When I get nervous I don't sweat or shake or anything but I always feel like I've got to go to the bathroom. I asked the receptionist where to go and when I came out Ma said, 'It's our turn . . . I better put some drops in your eyes before we go in. They're a little bloodshot.' She opened her bag.

'Not now, Ma!' I told her, glancing at the receptionist.

'Deenie Fenner . . .' she called.

Me and Ma stood up and the receptionist showed us into a small office. The walls were covered with pictures of beautiful girls. A lady was sitting behind a big glass-topped desk. 'Are you Deenie?' she asked.

'Yes,' I answered.

6

She held out her hand. 'I'm Mrs Allison.'

My mother reached over and shook hands with her. 'I'm Thelma Fenner, Deenie's mother.'

Mrs Allison smiled at me. She had a space between her two front teeth. 'So you want to be a model . . .' she said.

'Yes.'

Ma said, 'I have her portfolio right here, Mrs Allison.' She handed it to her.

Mrs Allison opened it up to the first page. 'What a sweet baby,' she said.

I felt my face turn red. I wish Ma would get rid of that picture.

'That's Deenie when she was sixteen months old,' Ma said. 'She's won a national contest and had her picture in all the magazines, advertising baby food.'

'Have you worked as a model since then, Deenie?' Mrs Allison asked.

'No,' I told her. 'My father didn't want me to at least until I started junior high. I'm in seventh grade now.'

'Modelling *is* hard work,' Mrs Allison said. 'I don't blame your father.' She flipped through my portfolio.

I wiggled my toes around inside my shoes. The big toe on my left foot hurt bad. I think I cut my toenails wrong again. They're always getting ingrown and infected.

When Mrs Allison was through looking at my pictures she zipped up my portfolio and said, 'You're a pretty girl, Deenie.'

'Thank you,' I said.

'Let's see you walk around the room.'

I glanced at Ma but she just smiled at me. I got up and walked across the room. The worst part of these interviews is having people stare at you while you walk around. I feel like a real klunk. When I finished crossing the room I stood in front of Mrs Allison's desk and turned around in a slow circle, the way Ma taught me.

Mrs Allison stood up and walked around her desk. She put her hands on my shoulders. 'Relax Deenie,' she said. 'You're too stiff.' She moved my head back and forth and kind of rearranged my shoulders. 'Now, try walking this way. You'll be more comfortable.'

I crossed the room again. I saw Mrs Allison make some notes on her pad. Then I stood in front of her and waited.

Mrs Allison looked at me without saying anything, and I was sure if I stood there for one more minute I would have to go to the bathroom again. I shifted from one foot to the other while I waited for her to say something.

Finally she said, 'I don't know, Deenie. There's something about the way you move that's not quite right. But your face is very lovely and you do photograph well. Let me think about you for a while. I'll be in touch.'

Mrs Allison stood up then and held her hand out to me. I shook it this time while Ma grabbed my portfolio off her desk.

'Thank you for coming, Mrs Fenner,' Mrs Allison told Ma. 'And for bringing Deenie.'

My mother nodded and took my arm, leading me out of the office. All the way down in the elevator Ma held on to my arm and she didn't say anything, not one word. When we were on the street she steered me into a lunchroom. We sat opposite each other, in a booth. Ma ordered a cheeseburger for each of us and when the waitress was gone I said, 'I'm sorry, Ma.'

'It looked like you slouched on purpose, Deenie.'

'I didn't, Ma. Honest. Why would I do that? I tried as hard as I could.' Tears came to my eyes.

'Don't give me that, Deenie. You heard Mrs Allison say there's something funny about the way you move.'

'Please, Ma . . . please believe me . . . I didn't do it on purpose.'

My mother didn't say anything for a minute. I took a sip of water. Finally, Ma said, 'Deenie, God gave you a beautiful face. Now He wouldn't have done that if He hadn't intended for you to put it to good use.'

'I know it, Ma.'

'I hope so. Because I'm not going through this again. Next time we have an appointment you'll have to try harder.'

'But Mrs Allison didn't say *no* to us, Ma. She said she'd think about me, remember?'

'That means *no*, Deenie. So we'll have to try another agency.'

'Can't we wait a little while? Maybe until next year?'

'Don't be silly,' Ma said. 'We don't want to waste time when you're ready now.' She reached out and patted my hand. 'I know this is hard for you, Deenie, but some day you'll thank me. You'll see.'

When the waitress brought our lunch I didn't feel like eating anything, but one thing that makes Ma really mad is seeing good food go to waste.

Chapter 2

That night I soaked my foot for an hour. My big toe was killing me. Midge called to ask how I made out at the modelling agency.

'It was okay,' I said.

'Me and Janet went to Woolworth's. She tried on orange lipstick and brown eyeshadow.'

'Did she get caught?'

'Of course not.'

When we go to Woolworth's Janet's the best at trying on junk without buying. You're not supposed to do that but Janet always gets away with it. The one time I tried on some nail polish the saleslady caught me and I had to buy the whole bottle.

'*And* we saw Harvey Grabowsky,' Midge said.

'You did?'

'Yes. We followed him all around the store.'

'Did he say anything?'

'He never even noticed.'

'Oh.'

Harvey is the best-looking guy in ninth grade. He's also on the football team and President of his class. Harvey has never said one word to me. I guess he doesn't talk to seventh-grade girls at all.

As soon as I hung up the phone rang again. It was Janet.

'We followed Harvey Grabowsky in Woolworth's,' she said.

'I know. I just talked to Midge.'

'Did she tell you what he bought?'

'No . . . what?'

'Three ballpoint pens and a roll of Scotch tape.
And once I stood right next to him and touched
his shirt sleeve!'

I just knew I'd miss out on something great by
going to New York.

Monday morning I got up early so I wouldn't have
to rush. I wanted to make sure I looked my best
because of cheerleading tryouts that afternoon.
Most times I don't even think about the way I look
but on special occasions, like today, being good-
looking really comes in handy. Not that a person
has any choice about it. I'm just lucky.

The only girl I know who's not trying out for
cheerleading is Midge. She would rather be *on* the
football team. No kidding, she's tough! And she's
the biggest kid in seventh grade, boys and girls
included. When she gets to ninth grade if they
don't let her try out football she's going to court to
sue the school for sexual discrimination. I used
to think that meant something else but now I know
the truth. In fifth grade we had a gym teacher who
never gave the girls a chance to shoot baskets. I

wish I had known about sexual discrimination then.

Me and Janet have been practising our cheers in her garage for two weeks. My mother doesn't know anything about it. She'd kill me. A lot of the games are on Saturdays and if I make the squad she won't be able to drag me around to any more modelling agencies. I'm counting on Daddy to make Ma understand . . . I'd really like to be a cheerleader *and* a famous model. If only getting to be a model wasn't so much trouble. It would be fun to see my face in some magazine, if it could get there without my going through all those dumb interviews!

By the time I got down to the kitchen Ma had my orange juice ready and an egg in to boil. Daddy is never around in the morning. He leaves the house before the rest of us get up. He's got a gas station on Rahway Avenue and he opens for business at six-thirty.

'You look special this morning,' Ma told me.

'I do?'

'Yes, you do.'

'Thanks, Ma.'

'Drink all your juice. Vitamin C is very important.'

'I'm drinking it.'

My mother makes sure I have breakfast every single day. She's really fussy about what I eat. She leaves Helen alone but watches me like a hawk. She thinks if she's in charge of my diet I'll never get pimples or oily hair. I hope she's right. Helen has a little of both and so does her best friend, Myra Woodruff. Aunt Rae says they're in the awkward stage.

As soon as I cracked my egg Helen walked into the kitchen. She doesn't talk in the morning. And she doesn't eat breakfast either. She just sucks on an orange and drinks coffee.

A car horn tooted outside. It was Myra's father who gives Helen a ride to the high school. She took one gulp of coffee and ran out the front door.

I meet Midge at her corner every morning. We catch the bus together. Her father's our family dentist but he didn't put Helen's braces on. He sent her to an orthodontist for that. She's through with her braces now and Daddy's glad because braces are very expensive. He used up his whole savings account paying for them. I know because I heard Ma tell that to Aunt Rae. Helen's teeth look pretty good. They're very straight and she's always brushing them.

Our town doesn't have school buses, except for the one that picks up the handicapped kids. They come to our school from all over because we have a Special Class. Gena Courtney, who lives on my street, takes that bus. We were in first grade together until her accident. She was hit by a delivery truck. Now she wears braces on her legs and she's blind in one eye. I always feel funny when I pass her house – like I should stop and say hello – but then I think I better not, because I wouldn't know how to act or anything.

We get student discount tickets to use on the public bus. Janet gets on a few stops after me and Midge, so we always save her a seat. When she got on this morning she came running back to where we were and as soon as she sat down she opened her purse and pulled out a raw chicken's foot. She poked me and Midge with it – so naturally we screamed because who'd want to be touched by that! So the old grouch bus driver yelled, 'Shut up back there or I'll put you off!' Janet put her chicken's foot away.

'Why are you carrying that thing around with you, anyway?' Midge asked her.

'For good luck,' Janet said.

'A *rabbit's* foot means good luck, stupid,' I told her.

'I can't carry one of those around,' Janet said. 'Rabbits aren't kosher. And I need something to bring me good luck this afternoon. I'm so nervous about tryouts I'm sick to my stomach.'

'Does your father know you swiped a chicken's foot?' Midge asked.

'I didn't swipe it. He gave it to me.'

Janet's father is a butcher and his store is right

near Daddy's gas station. There are Hebrew letters on the window. Janet says they're just to let people know that he's a kosher butcher. One time me and Midge called for Janet at her father's store. Mr Kayser had just gotten in a whole batch of dead turkeys. They were the ugliest things I'd ever seen. They weren't packaged nice like in the super-market. They just looked like dead birds with feathers and everything. But the worst part was when Mr Kayser reached inside one and pulled out this disgusting mess of gutsy stuff and some of it was purple! Me and Midge thought we'd vomit right on the sawdust but Janet just laughed and laughed.

We got to school just as the last bell rang. We said goodbye until lunchtime and headed for our formrooms. Mine's on the second floor. Susan Minton was waiting at my desk. She's always hanging around me. She says a lot of people think we look alike. I can't see it at all but whatever way I wear my hair Susan wears hers. And today she had her shirt buttoned up the back, the way I wore mine last Friday.

'I can't wait for this afternoon, Deenie,' Susan said, while I put my books in my desk. 'Aren't you excited about tryouts?'

'Not especially,' I said. I would never tell her the truth.

'Everybody thinks you're going to make the squad.'

'That's silly,' I said.

'But everybody thinks so anyway.'

I can't stand Susan and the way she talks. One time I complained about her at home and Ma said it's just that Susan looks up to me and I should feel flattered. But I don't. She's such a pain! And I don't think it's a compliment that she's always copying me either. I wish she wasn't in my form.

All morning I thought about cheerleading tryouts and I went over my cheers and jumps a thousand times in my mind, so I didn't hear Mr Fabrini when he called on me in English and he said I should stop dreaming about what I was going to eat for lunch and start paying attention.

Some days I bring my lunch from home and other days I buy it. It all depends on what Ma's got in the refrigerator. Today there wasn't anything good so I stood on line to buy the school lunch.

Midge usually gets to the cafeteria before me and Janet so she saves us a place. She brings the same lunch every day – two hard-boiled eggs. But all she eats is the white part – the yolks wind up in the garbage.

Harvey Grabowsky always sits at one special table over in the corner. Nobody would dare sit there unless Harvey said it was okay. And he never waits on line for his lunch either. He's got a bunch of girls who do everything for him. Those girls are really stupid! I would never stand on line for the privilege of bringing Harvey Grabowsky his lunch. I wouldn't even do it for Buddy Brader, unless he asked me very nicely and had a good reason, like a broken leg or something.

When I carried my lunch over to where Midge and Janet were sitting I saw Buddy and two of his friends were at the next table. As I sat down he called, 'Hey Deenie . . .'

I said, 'Oh, hi Buddy,' and I shook my hair the way Deenie in the movie did when she talked to her Bud. Then I felt my face get hot so I looked away and started to eat. But it's hard to swallow when there's somebody staring at you and I'm pretty sure Buddy Brader was staring at me all through lunch.

Chapter 3

At three o'clock I ran for the Girls' Room and so did everybody else. It was mobbed with all the kids who were going to tryouts. I didn't bother forcing my way close to the mirror. I went downstairs and when I passed the Special Class they were lining up to leave so I looked the other way. They give me a creepy feeling. I'm always scared Gena Courtney will see me and say something and I won't know what to say back.

I met Janet outside the auditorium. We waited a few minutes to make sure we wouldn't be the first ones going in. Then we walked down the aisle and found two seats in the middle of the fourth row.

The three judges were already there: Mrs Rappoport, Mr Delfone and Mrs Anderson. Mrs Rappoport is the girls' gym teacher. She really likes us — you can tell by the way she talks — she never raises her voice. And she doesn't make a big thing out of how clean our sneakers are either.

Mr Delfone is the boys' gym teacher and Mrs Anderson is the vice-principal of our school. As far as I know her only job is deciding what to do with kids who are discipline problems because if you make trouble you get sent to Mrs Anderson's office and sometimes you have to sit on the bench outside for a long time.

At three-fifteen Mrs Rappoport stood up and said, 'We're ready to begin now. Remember, girls, we'd love to choose every one of you but we can only pick one seventh grader, two eighth graders and three girls from ninth grade, so if you don't make it, don't feel too badly. There are so many other activities at Adams Junior High.'

Me and Janet squeezed hands. Hers felt cold and clammy. I pressed my legs tight together hoping I wouldn't get so nervous that I'd have to leave to go to the bathroom.

Mrs Rappoport said, 'We're going to call on you alphabetically and you can each do one cheer. After this round we'll decide on fifteen finalists.'

I looked around the auditorium. That meant most of us wouldn't even make the finals.

The first girl called was Alice Applebaum, a ninth grader. She went up on to the stage and did the same cheer I was going to do, spelling out the school name, first very slow, then faster, and finally very fast, with a big jump and a *Yea Team* at the end. She was really good and I was sure she would make it.

Four girls went before Mrs Rappoport called, 'Wilmadeene Fenner.' I stood up thinking this was almost as bad as at the modelling agency. Janet

20

whispered, 'Good luck, Deenie,' and we squeezed hands again.

I ran to the front of the auditorium because that's what Alice Applebaum did and I figured she knew the ropes. I went up the stairs and out on to the stage. I didn't look at the judges or the other girls because I knew if I did I'd never be able to go through with it. I just stood there clearing my throat like an idiot and then I began.

A . . . D . . . A . . . M . . . S

A. D. A. M. S.

ADAMS

Adams Adams

Junior High

Yea team!

I jumped as high as I could but my head didn't come close to touching my feet like Alice Applebaum's did. Still, I thought I'd done okay and when I passed Susan Minton on the way back to my seat she whispered, 'You were great, Deenie.' For once I was glad she thought so.

About forty minutes later Mrs Rappoport announced the fifteen finalists and Janet made it but I didn't. I pretended I was really happy for her. We hugged and everything before she said, 'I was sure it would be you, Deenie.'

I couldn't even answer her because I knew if I

did I'd start crying so I just shook my head and tried to smile. I sat there all through the finals, not wanting to, but what would Janet think if I walked out on her?

I was hoping that Janet wouldn't make it. I wanted the other seventh grader who made the finals to win. Then me and Janet could be unhappy together.

But when Mrs Rappoport announced the judges' decision Janet was the seventh grader they picked and I had to act like I was really happy for her all over again.

She said, 'I have to call my mother right away. Oh, Deenie . . . I'm so excited! I wish we both could have made it.'

I managed to say, 'Sure.'

Janet went to the phone booth outside the auditorium and while she was telling her mother the good news I knocked on the door and said I couldn't wait because I had to meet Helen at my father's gas station which was a big lie, but I couldn't face riding home on the bus with Janet.

Chapter 4

I took the bus to Daddy's gas station, knowing that Helen wouldn't be there because on Mondays and Wednesdays she works at the library after school. Daddy wasn't out front so I dumped my books on the counter inside and looked in the garage. He was working away underneath a station wagon. The second I saw him I started to cry. I knew I would. I'd been holding it in so long it felt good. I ran to him sobbing. 'Oh, Daddy . . .'

He slid out from under the wagon and said, 'Deenie . . . what is it?' When he stood up I grabbed hold of him and buried my face in his uniform. It smelled nice, like gasoline. I cried hard.

After a minute, Daddy held me away. 'Deenie, what's wrong?'

'I didn't make the cheerleading squad.' I could hardly get the words out.

Daddy sighed and said, 'Is that why you're so upset?'

I nodded. 'They chose Janet instead of me.'

Daddy smoothed my hair. 'Well, there'll be other times for you to try.'

'No there won't. This is it!'

'So you'll find another activity.'

He sounded like Mrs Rappoport. When I was

23

all cried out Daddy gave me the key to the Ladies' Room and told me to wash my face and he'd drive me home.

'Please don't tell Ma I was trying out. She'd probably kill me.'

'I won't say a word to anyone,' Daddy said. 'Now go and fix yourself up.'

I walked outside and around the back to the Ladies' Room. I splashed some water on my face.

'That's much better,' Daddy said, when I came back. I hung the key on the wall and grabbed my books off the counter. Daddy and I walked outside together.

'I have to tell Joe to close up for me,' Daddy said, unlocking our car.

'I'll wait here.' I got in and slouched way down in my seat. I didn't want Joe to see that I'd been crying. Joe Roscow has worked for Daddy since June when he finished high school, and from the first day Helen met him she's been hanging around the gas station. He's only going to be here for one year because he's saving his money to go to Forest Ranger School in Oregon. I don't know what Helen sees in him except that he's friendly and he wipes everybody's windshield without them having to ask, which Daddy says makes for good business.

When we got home Ma and Aunt Rae were in the kitchen. Aunt Rae's not my real aunt. We just call her that because she and Ma have been best friends for years. Her kids are all grown and married and it makes me feel funny to think that Daddy and Ma could have kids that old too. Ma says she and Daddy wanted babies in the worst way but it took fourteen years for God to bless them.

Ma was surprised to see Daddy home so early. She said, 'Frank . . . what's the matter?'

My father told her, 'Deenie dropped by so I decided I might as well drive her home and let Joe close up.'

'I'd better get supper started then. As soon as Helen comes home we can eat. Why don't you stay, Rae?'

Aunt Rae said, 'Thanks, Thelma, I think I will.'

Aunt Rae's face reminds me of an owl. Even when I was a little kid I thought so, but I never told her. Not that there's anything wrong with looking like an owl. It's just that Aunt Rae might not think that's a compliment.

'How come you're so quiet today, Deenie?' Aunt Rae asked.

'I don't know.'

'You look like you've been crying,' she said. 'Thelma, doesn't she look like she's been crying?'

Ma squinted at me. 'Deenie, what's wrong with your eyes? They're all bloodshot.'

'Nothing, Ma.'

'You're sure?'

'Yes, Ma.'

'You better let me put some drops in them.'

'I don't want drops, Ma!'

'Thelma . . .' Daddy put his hands on Ma's shoulder. 'She's okay. Just let her be.'

Aunt Rae said, 'Well . . . we've got some news to cheer you up, Deenie. You have an appointment to see the head of one of the top modelling agencies in New York.'

'I do?' I asked Ma.

'Thanks to Aunt Rae,' Ma said. 'She sent your picture in without telling us. Today they called to say they want to see you.'

'They do?'

'A week from Friday, at two o'clock,' Aunt Rae said.

'But that's when I have French.'

'So you'll take the afternoon off,' Ma said.

'I can't. I can't miss French. I'll never be able to make it up.'

'Deenie . . .' Ma said. 'I don't think you understand. This is a very important interview.'

'I don't care,' I said. 'I'm not going to miss French.'

Aunt Rae stood up. 'I just remembered I have leftover chicken in the refrigerator. I think I'll go home for supper after all.'

When she was gone Ma said, 'That wasn't a very nice way to act in front of Aunt Rae.'

'I'm sorry.'

'I hope so,' Ma told me. 'Because Aunt Rae is very good to you.'

'I said I'm sorry!'

'I heard Janet made cheerleading,' Helen said at supper.

'Yes,' I told her.

'Well . . . don't feel too bad . . . I didn't make it either and I tried out all three years I was at Adams.'

'Who says I care one way or the other?' I took a sip of milk.

'Deenie has more important things to think about than cheerleading,' Ma said.

'But she tried out,' Helen told Ma.

Ma put her pork chop down. 'That was a waste of time, Deenie. Suppose you had been picked? You would have had to tell them you couldn't do it. You can't give up all that time. You'll be working soon.' She reached for the salt.

'I didn't try hard, Ma. I just did it to keep Janet company.' I glanced at Daddy but he kept on eating.

'Cheerleading's a big thing at Adams,' Helen told Ma. 'Practically all the seventh grade girls try out. Don't you remember how much I wanted to make it then?'

'With your brain you don't need to jump around yelling cheers!' Ma said.

Daddy finished his apple sauce. 'I can understand why the girls try out,' he said. 'It makes them feel important to be on the cheerleading team.'

'Squad,' Helen said. 'They don't call it team. They call it squad.'

'Same difference,' Daddy said.

'As if Deenie needed to be a cheerleader to feel important. Just wait until her picture's on the cover of some magazine.' Ma waved her fork at me. 'I want you in bed by eight every night this week, Deenie.'

'But Ma . . .'

'You heard me. I don't want to take you on this interview with circles under your eyes. And you've got to practise walking an hour a day. Remember the last time . . . what that woman said?'

'Okay . . . okay . . .'

'Did you hear about Janet?' I asked Midge the next morning.

'Naturally. She called as soon as she got home. She was really excited.'

'She did just great,' I said. 'I knew the second she finished her cheer she'd make it. Did she tell you how I messed up?'

'No, what happened?' Midge asked.

'Oh, I flubbed my words and practically fell over backwards doing my jump. It was a riot! I almost cracked up right on the stage.' I laughed as hard as I could.

'Janet didn't tell me that.'

'I guess she didn't notice because she was nervous herself. But it was *so* funny. Anyway, I couldn't have accepted even if they'd picked me. You know I have all these interviews coming up. I really just tried out to keep Janet company.'

Midge didn't answer that because the bus came along then. We saved Janet a seat as usual, but when we got to her stop she wasn't waiting and we made it to school just as the first bell rang so we had to go straight to our formrooms. I wondered if Janet was sick. She seemed fine yesterday. Or maybe she was so excited she couldn't sleep last night and missed the bus.

Susan Minton was waiting by my desk in the form-room. 'I looked for you yesterday, after tryouts.'

'I had to go somewhere,' I said.

'Oh. I wanted to tell you what an awful mistake the judges made. They should have picked you. I just can't understand it.'

'Forget about it, will you, Susan!'

'Sure, Deenie . . . if you want me to. It's just that everybody thinks you should have made it. I mean, Janet's okay and all, but she isn't anything special.'

'I said, just forget it! Janet's one of my best friends.'

'I know it,' Susan said. 'And you must be really happy for her.'

'That's a fact.' I took a book out of my desk and pretended to read.

I didn't see Janet until lunchtime. She was waiting for me in the cafeteria. I said, 'Hi . . . I thought you were sick or something.'

'Oh no. Alice Applebaum called last night to say her mother drives her to school three days a week and since she lives near me she offered me a ride. Especially since we'll be practising together and all that.'

'Oh.'

'We're getting our sweaters and skirts this afternoon.'

'That's nice.'

'Deenie . . . I wish we both could have made the squad.'

'Look,' I told her, 'even if I had made it I'd have to quit because my mother's lined up a lot of interviews for me and I just wouldn't have time for modelling and cheerleading too.'

'You know something? I think I made the squad because I had that chicken's foot in my purse. It really brought me good luck!' Janet opened her purse and pulled it out.

'You still have it?'

'Yes . . . but now I'm giving it to you. If you carry it on your next interview it'll bring *you* good luck!'

Janet handed it to me. I didn't want to touch it but I didn't want to insult her either. So I took some napkins, wrapped it up, and stuck it in my purse.

Chapter 5

I have gym on Tuesdays and Thursdays right after lunch. I like having it then because it makes the afternoon go fast since there's only one period left after gym and that's when I have French.

Our French teacher, Madame Hoffman, won't let us speak one word of English while we're in her room. And that means not one! On the first day of school I had to go to the Girls' Room and Madame Hoffman wouldn't let me out of her class until I could say, 'May I please be excused?' in French. I almost died because by the time I learned to say it I wasn't sure I would make it to the Girls' Room in time. And the boys were all laughing at me too. I'm taking Spanish next year.

Midge and Janet aren't in my gym class but Susan Minton is. Whenever we have to take a partner she's always right there grabbing for my hand. This year we have modern dance. Starting in February we'll have sports. Then we won't have to take partners so often.

I was so busy thinking about how to get out of being Susan's partner that I didn't even care that the Creeping Crud was getting changed next to me. Her real name is Barbara Curtis but I named her the Creeping Crud because she's got this disgusting rash all over her. It's supposed to be some kind of allergy but who wants to take the chance of finding out by touching her? It could be leprosy or something like that! When we have to take partners in gym she's always the one who's left over and Mrs Rappoport says, 'Barbara, would you like to be my partner?'

I guess that's what would have happened today if I hadn't been so pokey getting dressed. But by the time I made it to the gym everyone had a partner, even Susan Minton. And since somebody was absent there was an even number of us today. So I wound up with Barbara Curtis and I had to do my warm-up exercises next to her, which wouldn't have been all that bad except when we were through Mrs Rappoport said, 'Okay, girls . . . now join hands with your partner and we'll practise our polka-step around the gym.'

I kept my hands behind my back until the music began.

'It's not catching,' Barbara said. 'It's just eczema.'

'I know that,' I told her.

'You act like you're scared to touch me.'

'Don't be silly,' I said and I grabbed her hand. It felt very rough, like sandpaper.

'And hop, step together, close . . .' Mrs Rappoport repeated as she clapped to the music. 'That's it . . . one, two, three . . . and hop, two, three . . . now spin your partner . . . very nice . . .'

When the bell rang I let go of Barbara's hand and ran for the row of sinks where I washed myself all over and lathered my hands at least six times.

At the end of the day, right before dismissal, Miss Greenleaf, my formroom teacher, called me up to her desk and handed me a note. It said:

Please send Deenie Fenner to see me in the gym after school.
Thank you.

Eileen Rappoport

It must be about cheerleading, I thought. Somebody must have quit and I'm going to be her replacement. Janet was right − her chicken's foot did bring me good luck!

Midge was waiting for me in the hall downstairs but I told her I had to see Mrs Rappoport.

'What do you have to see her about?' Midge asked.

'I'm not sure,' I said. I didn't want to tell her the good news yet.

'Should I wait?'

'If you want . . . and if I'm going to be long then I'll come tell you and you can go home without me.'

I ran down to the gym and said, 'Hi, Mrs Rappoport. You wanted to see me?'

'Oh, yes Deenie. I'd like to talk to you about something.'

I smiled.

Mrs Rappoport ran her hand through her hair which is bright reddish-orange. She said, 'I noticed it yesterday, when you were trying out for cheerleading, and again today, during gym class.'

What was she talking about? Maybe it didn't have anything to do with cheerleading after all.

'What is it?' I asked, thinking it might have something to do with Susan Minton — about her wanting to be my friend and me not being very nice to her. Or did Mrs Rappoport notice that I didn't want to hold hands with the Creeping Crud? Maybe I was going to get a lecture about that.

'I want you to bend over and touch your hands to your toes, Deenie.'

I did what Mrs Rappoport told me, all the time trying to figure out what touching my hands to my toes had to do with Susan Minton or the Creeping Crud unless this was how Mrs Rappoport punished kids who weren't nice to other people instead of sending them to Mrs Anderson's office to sit on the bench.

Mrs Rappoport circled around me a few times. Then she said, 'Okay, Deenie . . . you can stand up again. This time I'd like you to walk across the room slowly.'

As soon as she said that I knew it wasn't Susan

34

Minton or Barbara Curtis that Mrs Rappoport wanted to see me about. And it didn't have anything to do with cheerleading either. Which is why I suddenly shouted, 'It's my posture, isn't it? That's why I didn't make cheerleading. That's why I didn't even make the finals!'

'That has something to do with it, Deenie,' Mrs Rappoport said. 'Do you know your skirt is longer on one side than the other . . . and it was the same way yesterday, during tryouts.'

'I told my mother about that but she says it's because I slouch. What should I do . . . walk with books on my head for ever?'

'No, nothing like that. There could be some exercises that might help, though. I'll be in touch with your parents about it. We'll talk more another time. You run along now . . . and thanks for stopping by.'

Midge was waiting for me outside. 'That didn't take very long,' she said. 'What'd Mrs Rappoport want?'

'Something about my posture,' I told her.

'What about it?'

'I'm not sure. Do you think I have bad posture?'

'I never noticed. Let me see you walk.'

I walked a few feet and turned around. 'Well . . . did you notice anything?'

'Nope. You look just the same as always.'

'My mother's going to kill me. She'll say I'm slouching on purpose.'

'So don't tell her.'

'Don't worry . . . I won't. But Mrs Rappoport's going to call. She said she'd be in touch with my parents.'

'Maybe she'll write them a letter.'

'Maybe . . . but either way my mother's going to be plenty sore. You can't be a model if you don't have good posture.'

'So you can be something else.'

'Try and tell that to my mother!' I opened my purse, pulled out the chicken's foot and dumped it into the trash can on the corner.

Chapter 6

Every night after supper Helen takes off for Myra Woodruff's house. They do their homework together. I can't believe my sister has that much studying to do. Nobody expects much from my schoolwork so I get by with hardly ever cracking a book as long as I don't bring home any D's or F's.

Ma says Helen is excused from helping with the dishes because she works at the library twice a week and she baby-sits every weekend, so she needs all the studying time she can get. I'm *never* excused from helping in the kitchen. Ma usually does the washing and I dry everything and if, God forbid, I put something away that's just a teensy bit wet I never hear the end of it. My mother's very fussy about the kitchen. Well, she's fussy about the whole house. She spends hours and hours cleaning the place. She says our floors are so clean you could eat off them, not that anybody is thinking about doing that, but you could. One thing I'm sure of is I don't want to spend my life cleaning some house like Ma. Sometimes I think Helen's lucky. She'll be a doctor or lawyer or engineer and she'll never have to do those things. But if I don't make it as a model, then what?

The phone rang just as I was putting away the

37

last pot. I hollered, 'I'll get it,' and ran to the front hall.

It was Mrs Rappoport. I recognized her voice right away and she knew mine too because she said, 'Hello Deenie. May I speak to your mother or your father please.'

I thought about which one I should call to the phone and decided on Daddy. If Mrs Rappoport was going to discuss my posture Ma might get upset.

'Who is it?' Daddy asked, when I told him there was a phone call.

'It's Mrs Rappoport, my gym teacher,' I said, covering the mouthpiece with my hand.

I stood right next to my father while he said, 'Hello, this is Frank Fenner.'

After that he didn't say anything except a couple of 'uh huhs' and one 'yes, I see'. He motioned for me to go away so I went back to the kitchen, wondering exactly what Mrs Rappoport was telling him.

'Who was on the phone?' Ma asked.

'Mrs Rappoport, my gym teacher.'

'What does she want?'

'I'm not sure,' I said.

Ma sprinkled some cleanser into the sink. 'Did you do something wrong?'

'No, Ma . . . nothing like that.'

She rinsed the sink clean. 'Then why is she calling here?'

'I don't know.'

'Well,' Ma said, putting down the dish towel. 'I better find out.'

Daddy was hanging up when we got to the hall.

'What was that all about?' Ma asked him.

'When was the last time Deenie had a check-up at Dr Moravia's office?' Daddy said.

'In April,' Ma told him. 'She had to have one before junior high. Why?'

Daddy looked at me. I don't think he wanted to say anything else but he did. 'It seems that Mrs Rappoport thinks we should take her for another one.'

'What for?' Ma asked, turning towards me. 'Deenie, do you feel sick? Is there something you haven't told me?'

'No, Ma,' I said. 'I think it's my posture. That's all.'

'That's right,' Daddy said. 'Mrs Rappoport noticed it and thinks we should look into the situation. There might be some exercises that Dr Moravia could recommend.'

'You're talking in circles,' Ma said.

Daddy gave her a sharp look which meant he wasn't going to discuss it in front of me.

Ma said, 'Deenie, you promised to practise standing very straight and tall.'

39

'I tried,' I said.

'I don't think so,' Ma told me. 'I think you've got other things on your mind so you forget what's really important!'

'Thelma . . .' Daddy began.

'Frank, that girl has got to learn . . .'

'I don't want to talk about it any more,' I called, racing up the stairs.

I got undressed and stood in front of my mirror. Helen doesn't have a full–length mirror in her room but I let her use mine whenever she wants to see her whole self, which is practically never. I turned around and around, trying to see myself from all angles. There wasn't anything wrong with my posture! I wasn't round–shouldered and my stomach didn't stick out either. So what was Mrs Rappoport so excited about that she had to call my parents?

The next afternoon, when I got home from school, Ma said, 'We have to be at Dr Moravia's office by four. Aunt Rae's coming to pick us up in a few minutes. Go and wash your hands and face and make sure your underwear's clean with no rips.'

'Oh Ma! Who cares about my underwear?'

'I do,' Ma said. 'So get going.'

'Okay,' I told her, heading upstairs.

I don't mind Dr Moravia as long as I don't need a shot or that tine test which he always says will feel like a little mosquito bite, when it really feels more like a big bee sting. But I had that in April. So probably he'll give Ma a prescription for some vitamins and tell her to stop worrying because I'm just going through the awkward stage. Or maybe I'm going to get my period again. I had it once, last June. The booklet I sent for says when you start out it might be a long time before you get regular, like Helen. So maybe that's why my posture's funny. Except I never heard of bad posture as a symptom of getting your period. But if that's what it is then Ma can't be mad at me, so I hope it is.

My mother doesn't drive. Aunt Rae takes her every place she has to go. Or else she goes by bus. But since Aunt Rae has nothing better to do she doesn't mind driving Ma around. Especially since she has a new car. It's bright blue and Aunt Rae takes such good care of it I wouldn't dare spit my gum in the ashtray like I do when I ride with Daddy.

When we got to Dr Moravia's office there were three kids ahead of me. Ma's always saying the best place to pick up germs is waiting at the doctor's office. By now I know better than to sit near anybody who's coughing or looking sick.

At my last check-up Dr Moravia filled in a bunch of forms for junior high. I got weighed, measured and had my blood pressure taken first.

Then Dr Moravia looked into my eyes, up my nose and down my throat. He also listened to my heart.

This time when he called me into his office he told Ma to wait outside with Aunt Rae, instead of coming in with me.

'How's everything, Deenie?' Dr Moravia asked.

'Just fine,' I told him.

'Good . . . good . . . let's see how much you've grown. Step on to the scale please.'

'You've gained a half pound since last April and you're an inch taller,' Dr Moravia said, when he was done weighing and measuring me.

'Do you think I'm going to be huge?' I asked.

He laughed a little. 'You're going to be just right.'

'My mother wants me to be a model so it won't hurt if I get really tall.'

Dr Moravia smiled. 'Now Deenie . . . I'd like you to bend over and touch your hands to your toes.'

'My gym teacher made me do the same thing.'

Dr Moravia pressed his hand against my side.

'I really try to stand up straight,' I said.

'It has nothing to do with that,' he told me. 'You can come up now, Deenie.'

'It's not my posture?' I asked, straightening my clothes.

'No. It's your spine, I think. But I'm going to

send you over to see a friend of mine just to make sure. His name is Dr Griffith.'

'What's he going to do?'

'Oh, just take some X-rays and look you over.'

'You think something's broken?' I asked.

'No. But something might be growing the wrong way.'

'What do you mean?'

'Well, I can't say for sure, but Dr Griffith is a specialist – an orthopaedist – and he'll be able to find out exactly what the trouble is.'

'Do you think it's something bad?'

'Nothing that can't be fixed,' Dr Moravia said, opening the door to his office and calling my mother. 'Deenie, you can sit in the waiting room now. Your mother will be out in a minute.'

I sat down next to Aunt Rae. She was reading a magazine called *Today's Health*. She closed it as soon as she saw me and asked, 'What did he say?'

'I'm not sure,' I told her. 'Something about my spine.'

'Your spine?' Aunt Rae said.

'Yes . . . why . . . is that bad?'

'I don't know,' Aunt Rae told me. 'You're sure he said your spine?'

'Yes . . . I think so.' He did, didn't he? Now I was getting all mixed up. Or did he say my *tine*? Maybe my tine test came out wrong. But if that was so why didn't he give me another one back in April?

In a few minutes Ma came out of Dr Moravia's office, clutching a piece of paper. 'What's that?' I asked. 'Is it a prescription? Did you remind him I can't swallow pills?'

'It's nothing,' Ma said. 'It's just a doctor's name and address.'

'Oh . . . Dr Griffith . . . right? He's a friend of Dr Moravia's. Did you know that?'

Ma didn't answer me. She just said, 'Let's go.'

When we were in the car I asked, 'Well . . . what'd he tell you?'

'Nothing definite,' Ma said. 'We have to see Dr Griffith first.'

'But it's not my fault. He told you that, didn't he?'

Ma acted like she didn't hear me.

Aunt Rae said, 'Who wants to stop for a soda?'

Ma heard that because she said, 'Let's go home. We'll have something there.'

I said, 'Ma, didn't Dr Moravia tell you that it's not my fault?' I wanted to get that straight right away.

'Yes,' Ma said. 'Yes, he did tell me that.'

'Good! Now you can't be mad at me.'

'But I don't believe him,' Ma said.

'Then you do think it's my fault?'

'I didn't say that.'

'Then what?'

'I mean . . . doctors make mistakes all the time.'

44

Chapter 7

Dr Griffith's nurse called Wednesday night, saying that someone had cancelled an appointment for Thursday morning and that Ma should bring me in at nine-thirty.

I phoned Midge to tell her I wouldn't be at the bus stop because of an important appointment.

'Another interview?' she asked.

'No, a doctor's appointment.'

'Why? What's wrong?'

'I don't know . . . remember that business about my posture?'

'Yes.'

'Well . . . this doctor I have to see is an ortho-paedist.'

'That's a bone specialist.'

'How do you know?'

'Because last year, when I broke my arm, I had to go to an orthopaedist.'

'Dr Griffith?' I asked.

'No, Dr Littel. He was nice.'

'I wish I was going to him. At least you could tell me what he's like.'

'Don't worry. It probably won't even hurt.'

'I hope not. I'll let you know on Friday.'

'Okay. Bye.'

What really surprised me on Thursday morning was that Daddy didn't go to the gas station. Instead of Aunt Rae driving us to Dr Griffith's office, Daddy was going to take us himself, which is what gave me the idea that there was something really bad wrong with me because why else did Helen actually talk to me at breakfast? For somebody who was so sick I felt fine. I felt just like always. So I decided I must have one of those weird diseases where you never know anything's wrong with you until the end.

Dr Griffith's office is in the Medical Arts Building on West Jersey Street. We parked in the lot behind the building and took the elevator up to the third floor. The waiting room was full of people and most of them had some kind of cast on their arms or legs.

We sat in the waiting room until ten after ten when the nurse called my name. Daddy and Ma stood up with me and the nurse showed us into a little office where another nurse told us to sit down. Then she asked us a lot of questions which Daddy answered, things like our address and phone number and what kind of medical insurance we have. When she got to that question Daddy took some cards out of his wallet and showed her the numbers on them. She must have been a good typist because as Daddy answered her questions she typed everything out on yellow forms, without ever looking down at her fingers.

After that the first nurse came back and told my parents they could go sit in the waiting room and she would call them when the doctor was ready to talk. She took me into an examining room and told me to take off all my clothes except my underpants. Then she handed me this white paper thing made like a bathrobe. 'Tie it in the back, please. The doctor will be with you in a few minutes.' She left the room and closed the door behind her.

I didn't like the idea of getting undressed, but I did. The paper robe was so big I had to wrap it around myself twice. And when I walked it dragged all over the floor.

I waited for the doctor for twenty whole minutes. I know because I watched a big clock on the wall. It jumped every minute, same as the clocks in school. I checked everything in the room, wondering what Dr Griffith would do to me, if he ever showed up. There was a table of instruments but none of them looked too scary. A few looked like different-sized scissors. I didn't see any needles or knives, and was I glad! The stool I was sitting on turned around and around and I spent some time twirling on it until I got dizzy. Then I read all the diplomas on the wall. I found out Dr Griffith's first name is Harold. I also found out where he went to college, where he went to medical school and what year he got out of the army. There was an old-fashioned picture of a football team too. I wondered if one of those funny-looking guys was Dr Griffith.

Finally the door opened and this huge man walked in. He was wearing a white coat so I knew he was Dr Griffith. Another nurse was with him. She had a pin on her uniform saying MISS VERNON. 'Deenie . . . this is Dr Griffith,' she told me.

Dr Griffith closed the folder he'd been reading and put it down on the instrument table. 'Hello there,' he said. 'Let's see what Dr Moravia's talking about. Come over here please, Deenie.'

Dr Griffith is about twice as big as Dr Moravia and I've always thought Dr Moravia is pretty big himself. Dr Griffith looks like a giant. I don't see how he fits through doorways, he's so tall. I didn't move. I just sat there on my twirl-around stool and looked at him.

'Come on, Deenie. I'm not going to hurt you.'

'What are you going to do?'

'Just have a look,' Dr Griffith said.

'Really?' I asked, glancing at Miss Vernon. I couldn't tell anything from her expression. She was busy checking her fingernails.

'I promise,' Dr Griffith said.

I stood up and walked over to him. His hands looked big enough to squash a person right in half. He turned me away from him and untied my paper robe. Then he put his hands on my back. They were freezing cold. I tried to think of other things. I asked him, 'Were you ever a football player?'

'A long time ago,' Dr Griffith said, pressing on my back. 'When I was in high school.'

'I thought so. You're in that picture aren't you?' I asked him, pointing to the wall.

'Yes. Third row, seventh from the left. Would you put your hand down at your side please?'

'Oh, I'm sorry,' I told him.

'That's better.'

'Were you a good football player?'

'I was fair,' he said. 'Are you interested in football?'

'I'm not sure. I don't know much about it yet. I wanted to be a cheerleader, but I didn't make the squad.'

He didn't say anything about that. I thought he would. I thought he'd say, 'Well, you can try again next year' or something like that. Instead he said, 'Bend over and touch your toes with your hands, Deenie.'

'Why does everybody keep asking me to do that?'

'It's a good way for us to see if your hips are even,' Dr Griffith said.

'Suppose they're not?'

'If one is higher than the other it might indicate the problem.'

'Oh,' I said, wondering what that meant.

Dr Griffith pushed at my side. Then he told me to sit down on the turn-around stool and he looked me over from every angle.

'Now Deenie, lie down on the table please,' Dr Griffith said.

I climbed up on the examining table. Miss Vernon stood next to me and smiled.

'Legs out straight please,' Dr Griffith said.

'Are you going to hurt me?' I asked. 'I'm not scared but I'd rather know in advance.'

'I'm just going to measure you,' Dr Griffith said. I didn't believe him so I was really surprised when he held a tape measure to my right hip and measured me from there to my ankle. Then he went around to my other side and did the same thing.

'Do I measure okay?' I asked.

'Um . . .' Dr Griffith said, as he jotted something down in his folder. 'Now, one more thing, Deenie. Come down off the table and stand up straight.'

I jumped down from the table and stood as straight as I could. That's when Dr Griffith did the craziest thing – he came from behind, put his hands on the sides of my face and lifted me right off the floor.

'Put me down!' I said. 'I don't like that!'

'Sorry,' Dr Griffith told me, 'but it's important.'

He lowered me to the floor and moved me from side to side.

When he was done Miss Vernon asked, 'That wasn't so bad, was it, Deenie?'

I knew then that Dr Griffith must be through examining me.

'Okay,' Miss Vernon said. 'Follow me and I'll show you to the X-ray room.'

She led me down the hall until we came to a room marked *X-ray*. Another nurse was waiting for me there. She said, 'Hello Deenie, I'm Mrs Hall, the X-ray technician, and I'm going to take some pictures of you. You won't feel a thing, so just relax.'

Mrs Hall arranged me into certain positions and she was right, I didn't feel anything. It was just like having a regular picture taken. First she took X-rays of me standing up and then lying down on the table and bending to the side. Each time she got me ready she left the room to stand behind a door with a glass window in it and she'd say, 'Take a deep breath now . . . and hold it until I tell you to breathe again.'

All I heard was a little buzzer noise and then she'd say, 'Okay . . . relax.'

When she was done with me I got dressed and Miss Vernon came back to take me into an office with a nice orange rug. Daddy and Ma joined me there.

'How'd it go, Deenie?' Daddy asked.

'It didn't hurt,' I told him.

Dr Griffith opened the door and told us to make ourselves comfortable. He was carrying the same folder and when he sat down at his desk he spread it out in front of him. Finally he said, 'Well now . . . Dr Moravia was right. Deenie has adolescent idiopathic scoliosis.'

All I understood of that was adolescent and something that sounded like idiotic.

'What does that mean?' Daddy asked.

'It means she has a structural curvature of the spine which has a strong tendency to progress rapidly during the adolescent growth spurt. Let me show you something,' Dr Griffith said, taking an X-ray out of the folder. He stuck it up on some kind of screen on the wall and when he turned a switch it all lit up and the X-ray looked like a skeleton. He tapped a pencil to the X-ray. 'You see here . . .' he said. 'This is Deenie's spine. It demonstrates the curve and confirms my clinical diagnosis.'

'I don't understand,' Ma said. 'Why Deenie . . . of all people?'

'I can't answer that, Mrs Fenner. But there is a strong familial tendency.'

Ma shook her head. 'No one in my family has ever had anything like this. My family's always been very healthy.'

'I can't think of anyone either,' Daddy said.

'The important thing now is Deenie,' Dr Griffith said. 'Not who's to blame for her condition.'

'Am I going to die?' I asked.

'Deenie!' Ma said.

But I didn't care that she didn't like my question. So I asked it again. 'Well, am I?'

'Eventually we're all going to die,' Dr Griffith said. 'But not of scoliosis. I can promise you that.'

'Then what's the difference if I have it?'

'We have to correct the curve,' Dr Griffith said.

Daddy asked, 'What do you suggest, Doctor?'

'I suggest you see a scoliosis specialist,' Dr Griffith told him. 'I can recommend a good man to you.'

'Another doctor?' I asked.

'Yes.'

'But I don't want to see another doctor! Can't you just fix it up yourself?'

'No,' Dr Griffith said. 'I don't handle scoliosis cases.'

'What can be done for her?' Daddy asked.

'There are two choices,' Dr Griffith told him. 'Surgery or a brace.'

I stood up. 'Suppose I don't want either one,' I said in a very loud voice.

'We have to correct the curve,' Dr Griffith said again.

I was tired of listening to the same old line. So I asked him, 'Who says we have to correct it? Why not just leave it alone?'

'It has to be corrected for cosmetic reasons,' Dr Griffith told me.

'Cosmetic?' Ma said, before I had a chance to ask about it. 'What do you mean?'

'If the curve isn't corrected it will result in a spinal deformity,' Dr Griffith said.

'You're not telling us that Deenie's going to be deformed, are you?' Daddy asked, while Ma started whispering 'Oh my God,' over and over again.

'I'm saying her condition has to be corrected in order to prevent such a deformity,' Dr Griffith said. 'The sooner the better.'

In the car, on the way home, Ma told Daddy, 'Your cousin Belle had something wrong with her back . . . remember?'

'That was different,' Daddy said. 'She had a slipped disc.'

'But I'll bet that's where this came from.'

'I don't think so,' Daddy said.

'Because you don't want to think so!' Ma told him.

I wanted them to stop acting like babies and start helping me. I expected Daddy to explain everything on the way home – all that stuff Dr Griffith had been talking about – that I didn't understand. Instead, he and Ma argued about whose fault it was that I have something wrong with my spine until we pulled into our driveway. It was almost as if they'd forgotten I was there.

Chapter 8

As soon as Daddy unlocked the front door I ran upstairs.

'Deenie . . .' Ma called. 'Where are you going?'

'To my room.'

'Come have a snack with us.'

'I'm not hungry.' I closed my bedroom door and took the S volume of my encyclopedia down from the shelf. If Daddy wasn't going to explain any- thing to me then I'd have to find out about it myself.

I looked up scoliosis. It said: *Skoh lih OH sihs, means a side-to-side curve or bend of the normally straight spine or backbone. Scoliosis may occur in any part of the spine. It may be single (curved like a C) or double (curved like an S). Scoliosis starts in childhood or the teens. It has a strong familial tendency. Treatment includes exercises, braces or surgery.*

I copied all of that down in my notebook. I didn't understand the whole thing but I got the general idea. The next thing I looked up was spine. There was half a column, none of it very interesting. But under related articles it said *hunch- back*. So I slammed the book closed and reached for H. I copied down everything: *Hunchback is a severe rounded or sharp prominence of the upper part of the back. Because this part of the back sticks out like a big hump, the condition is sometimes called humpback. Hunchback is caused by any condition that deforms the bones of the upper part of the spine. Hunchback involves the portion of the spine to which the ribs are connected. The hump results when the front part of the spinal bones collapses, spreading the back part.*

The last part didn't make much sense but the rest of it was a good description of Old Lady Murray!

That night, when I was ready for bed, I read over what I'd written a few times before I made up my mind. I would have an operation! I'd let the doctors fix me up. So what if I missed a few weeks of school. It would still be better than wearing a brace or winding up like Old Lady Murray.

I ran downstairs to tell Daddy and Ma about my decision, but the kitchen door was closed and I could hear them talking. I stood next to the door and listened.

Ma said, 'No one's cutting Deenie open!'

'Thelma,' Daddy told her, 'he didn't say they'd have to operate.'

'I don't care what they say,' Ma answered. 'Nobody's cutting Deenie open. Doctors make mistakes all the time.'

'Stop fooling yourself!' Daddy said. 'The doctors are right about Deenie.'

'Even if they are I'm not letting them operate. Suppose they make a mistake while she's on the table? They could cut the wrong thing and she'll wind up a cripple. Is that what you want?'

'They probably won't have to operate. We'll see what Dr Kliner says. After all, he's a specialist.'

Ma started crying. 'My beautiful baby . . . my beautiful, beautiful baby.'

'Carrying on like this isn't going to help Deenie,' Daddy said.

'Oh Frank! I had such plans for her,' Ma said. 'I can't believe this is really happening.'

I turned away from the kitchen door and ran back to my room. As soon as I got into bed I started touching myself. I have this special place and when I rub it I get a very nice feeling. I don't know what it's called or if anyone else has it but when I have trouble falling asleep, touching my special place helps a lot.

The next day, in the cafeteria, I told Janet and Midge, 'I'm going to have an operation.'

'What?' Janet spat out a piece of ham. 'I don't believe it!'

'Is that why you went to the orthopaedist?' Midge asked.

I looked around to make sure no one else could hear, especially Buddy Brader, who was at the next table. Midge and Janet put their heads near mine and I talked very softly. 'I wouldn't want this to get around,' I said.

'Don't worry.'

'Our lips are sealed.'

'Well . . .' I looked around one more time but Buddy wasn't listening. He was fooling around with his friends. 'I have a crooked spine,' I whispered. 'And they have to operate to straighten it out.'

'No kidding!' Janet said.

'So it wasn't your posture?' Midge asked.

'No.'

'When are you going to the hospital?' Janet said.

'I don't know yet. I have to see one more doctor but I think it will be soon.'

'Which hospital?' Midge asked. 'General?'

'I don't know that either.'

'I hope we can visit you,' Janet said.

'You better!'

'But you have to be fourteen to visit patients,' Midge said.

'So? We can look fourteen,' Janet said. 'I'll just fix my hair like this . . .' She pulled all her hair up on top of her head. 'And I'll make an old-looking face like this . . .' Janet looked so silly me and Midge couldn't help laughing at her.

'Listen . . .' I told them, giving Midge a friendly punch in the arm, 'I like pink roses best!'

That night Janet called. 'Can you come downtown with me and Midge tomorrow?'

'To shop?'

'No . . . for lunch and a movie.'

'Hang on . . . I have to ask.' I put the phone down and went into the kitchen. Ma was finishing up the dishes. She said yes, I could go downtown with my friends.

We took the bus at ten-thirty so we'd have enough time to go exploring in Woolworth's before lunch, but at the last minute Janet and Midge decided to get off in front of Drummond's Department Store instead.

'Why are we getting off here?' I asked.

'To go shopping . . .' Midge said.

'But you said we weren't going to shop. I only brought $3.50 with me.'

'Don't worry,' Midge said.

Janet grabbed my arm. 'Come on, Deenie!' She pulled me through the revolving door and into the store. Then Midge took my other arm and both of them led me to the elevator. 'Fourth floor, please,' Midge told the operator.

'What's going on?' I asked.

'You'll see in a minute,' Janet said.

I tried to think of what could be on the fourth floor. 'Shoes?' I asked.

'Nope,' Janet said, starting to laugh.

The elevator door opened and we stepped out.

'Tell me what's happening!' I said.

'Soon . . . soon . . .'

We walked across the floor to a small department

called JUNIOR LINGERIE. There was a salesgirl behind the counter and Janet told her, 'We'd like to see something beautiful in a nightgown.'

'What size?' the salesgirl asked.

'For her,' Midge said, pointing at me.

I opened my mouth but before I could say anything Midge said, 'It's for the hospital . . . after your operation . . .'

'So you look pretty when we come to visit,' Janet added.

'I . . . I mean I . . . I don't . . .' I began.

'Don't say a word,' Janet said. 'That's what friends are for.' She turned to the salesgirl. 'She's having an operation . . . not that you'd know it to look at her, but she is.'

'Oh, I'm sorry,' the salesgirl said.

'She's going to be fine when it's over,' Janet told her.

'I'm sure she will,' the salesgirl said. 'What colour do you like?' she asked me.

'Ummm . . . pink,' I said. 'Either that or lavender.'

We looked through a pile of nighties before we found one made of two layers of the softest nylon. The top layer was pink and the underneath was purple so when you moved it around it had a sort of lavender look to it.

'That's perfect!' Janet said, holding it up to me.

'What do you think, Deenie?' Midge asked.

'It's beautiful!' I said. 'But it's $12.95.'

'Never mind about that,' Midge told me. 'We're charging it. As long as it's what you really want we don't care what it costs.'

'I love it!' I said, thinking that maybe Buddy Brader would visit me too.

'We'll take it,' Janet said. 'And we'd like it gift-wrapped because it's a present.'

When we were outside again I hugged Janet and Midge and told them, 'No girl could have better friends!'

Next we went to lunch but they wouldn't let me pay for anything even though I kept saying, 'But I have $3.50.'

'Save it,' Midge said. 'Everything's on us.'

'You're the guest of honour,' Janet said. 'And guess what movie we're taking you to see?'

'I don't know.'

'The one at the Rialto . . . it's X-rated.'

I started to laugh. 'But how can we get in? You have to be eighteen, at least.'

'We can pass for that with no trouble,' Janet told me. 'Just concentrate on looking old.'

But besides looking old you also had to prove you were at least eighteen and since we couldn't the lady in the booth wouldn't sell us tickets so we settled for the movie down the street which was called *Massachusetts General* and from the pictures outside we knew it was about a hospital.

There were two cartoons before the main picture and by that time we needed more popcorn so Midge went out to the lobby to buy it. When she came back she whispered, 'I just saw Buddy Brader and Steve Hildrick.'

'Where are they sitting?' I asked.

'I don't know. I saw them buying candy.'

'Did they see you?' Janet said.

'Sure,' Midge told her. 'I said hello to them.'

'Did they ask who you were with?' I said.

'No. They didn't say anything.'

I turned around in my seat but I couldn't find them anywhere.

'Are they by themselves or with a whole bunch of guys?' Janet asked.

'I don't know!' Midge said. 'What's the difference anyway?'

'None,' Janet told her.

I turned around again. Were they sitting nearby? Could they see us? I should have worn a clean sweater.

The picture started. The first scene was of this young doctor making out with a nurse. You knew it was a nurse because she still had on her white hat. Naturally we all laughed. The next scene showed a gory operation. I could still hear Ma saying, 'Nobody's going to cut Deenie open.'

Midge leaned across Janet and said, 'Maybe you shouldn't watch this part, Deenie.'

'It's all right,' I told her. 'My operation's not going to be like that.'

'They're not going to mess with Deenie's guts,' Janet whispered. 'Just her spine . . . isn't that right?'

'That's right,' I said.

Somebody sat down in the seat next to me then. I glanced over because Ma's told me a million times never to let a strange man sit next to me in the movies. If one does I'm supposed to get up and change seats and if the man should follow me I'm supposed to call the usher and report him.

Only it wasn't a strange man sitting next to me this time. It was Buddy Brader. When I looked over at him he was staring right at me. And he was kind of smiling too.

I said, 'Oh, hi, Buddy.'

Steve Hildrick was sitting next to him. So I whispered, 'Hi, Steve.'

They acted like they were really surprised to see me.

I tried very hard to concentrate on the movie but it wasn't easy. Pretty soon Buddy Brader put his arm around my chair and when he did, Janet, who was on my other side, gave me a kick and started to laugh. So I looked over at Buddy as if to say, 'What do you think you're doing?' and that's when he took his arm off the back of the seat and put it on my shoulder! After a few minutes of that he leaned close and whispered, 'Why don't you change seats with Steve?'

Janet, who was leaning just as close on my other side, said, 'Go ahead, Deenie.' I guess that meant she wanted to sit next to Steve. So I stood up and moved over while Steve sat down between Buddy and Janet. He put his arm around her right away. Not the chair, but *her*.

This time Buddy didn't do that. He reached down for my hand instead. I never held hands with a boy before. At least, never like that, in a dark place where you don't have to hold hands because you need a partner for any special reason, like dancing or something.

It felt very nice too. Buddy's fingers were warm. I didn't look at him once the whole time we were holding hands. But when the young doctor and nurse were going at it again he squeezed my fingers which made me look over at Janet to see if she noticed that I was holding hands, and I saw she and Steve were doing the same thing except he still had his other arm around her. Midge was still looking straight ahead at the movie.

Halfway through the picture I noticed that my hand was sweating. It was during the scene where the girl died on the operating table. You knew she was dead when the bleeps stopped and the lines didn't go up and down on the little machine any more. By then I really had to go to the bathroom.

I've never been able to make it through a whole show. Even when I was little Ma had to take me out a couple of times whenever we saw a movie. So I whispered, 'Excuse me,' to Buddy and he let go of my hand. When he did he wiped his own off on his pants.

I went to the Ladies' Room and when I was done I stopped to have a look in the mirror. If only I'd known I was going to meet Buddy Brader I'd have washed my hair.

When I got back to my seat Buddy picked up my hand again. I was hoping he would.

As soon as the picture was over we all walked outside together and then Buddy and Steve said, 'See you around,' and they took off.

I thought Buddy would say something more to me. And I guess Janet was kind of disappointed too because she called after them, 'Okay . . . see you around.'

Buddy and Steve turned and waved and me and Janet waved back.

Then the three of us walked to the bus stop. Midge didn't say a word all that time. When we got there she bought a pack of sugarless gum from Old Lady Murray but she didn't offer a piece to me or Janet.

I didn't look away from Old Lady Murray like usual. Instead, I said 'Hello' to her, which I've never done before. She said 'Hello' back and I could see her gold front tooth. She was wearing a black sweater with a rip in one sleeve and over that she had on a carpenter's apron with a million pockets where she kept her change. I studied the bump on her back and wondered if she always had it or if it grew there when she got older.

Our bus came and we got on and found three seats together. As soon as we sat down I told Janet how my hand sweated in the movies and how Buddy wiped it off on his pants and she told me that Steve let his hand rest over her shoulder like maybe he was trying to feel something else, but she didn't know what to do about it so she didn't do anything.

Midge listened to us and then right when Janet was telling me she's always liked Steve Hildrick secretly, Midge said, 'I think it's cheap to let boys sit next to you in the movies. Did you see how fast they got away as soon as we were outside? They were just interested in what they could get in the dark.'

'That's not so!' Janet said. 'You're just saying that because there were only two of them.'

'I am not!' Midge told her.

'Suppose Harvey Grabowsky sat down next to you and wanted to hold your hand,' Janet said. 'I'll bet anything you'd let him.'

'Those measly eighth graders aren't Harvey Grabowsky!' Midge practically shouted.

66

'You're just jealous!' Janet insisted.

'Jealous . . . ha!'

I didn't say anything because I knew the truth. Midge really was jealous and I didn't blame her. I held my gift-wrapped nightie close. It was too bad that Midge had helped plan such a nice day for me and now she was going home feeling worse than anybody. I hope the next time we meet Buddy Brader in the movies he's got at least two friends with him and that one of them will like Midge!

Chapter 9

Monday night I couldn't finish my supper.

'You need all your vitamins,' Ma said. 'Especially now.'

'I just don't feel hungry,' I said.

'I cooked all afternoon,' Ma told me.

'I'm sorry . . .'

'Oh, leave her alone for once!' Helen said.

'Since when are you her mother?' Ma asked.

'If I was I wouldn't pick on her the night before she has to see another doctor!'

'Nobody's picking on Deenie,' Daddy said. 'Ma's only saying she needs her strength.'

'And you should mind your manners, Helen Fenner,' Ma said.

'Besides,' Daddy said, 'Deenie's not worried about seeing Dr Kliner.'

'Of course she's not,' Ma said. 'Why should she be worried? Nobody's going to do anything to her.'

'Can I be excused?' I asked.

Later, Helen came to my room with a piece of cake and a glass of milk. 'If I had scoliosis I'd want to talk about it.' She put the cake on my desk and handed me the milk. 'But Ma's told me a million times not to mention it to you.'

'There's nothing to talk about,' I told her. 'I'm having an operation and then I won't have scoliosis any more.'

'I've been reading up on it at the library,' Helen said, 'and I don't think you're going to need an operation.'

'You're wrong, Helen. I do need one. I already told Janet and Midge. You want to see something?' I went to my dresser and opened the bottom drawer where I'd hidden my new nightie. I pulled it out and held it up. 'Midge and Janet gave it to me for when I go to the hospital.'

'It's beautiful,' Helen said, touching the material.

'Do you remember some cousin of Daddy's named Belle?' I asked.

'No.'

'Ma says I got my scoliosis from her.'

'She had it too?'

'No, but she had a bad back.'

'That probably doesn't have a thing to do with it.'

'That's what Daddy said, but Ma doesn't believe him.'

'Ma really burns me up sometimes!' Helen said. 'I wish Daddy would tell her off just once!'

On Tuesday morning I wasn't surprised that Daddy stayed home from work to drive me to my appointment. I expected him to. What did surprise me was that Dr Kliner's office is in New York and the building it's in looks more like an apartment house than an office. There was a black door with a brass knocker and when Daddy used it a nurse opened the door and said, 'Deenie Fenner?' How did she know I was me?

She showed us into a big living-room kind of place with lots of chairs and couches and tables and a fancy Chinese rug on the floor with fringes around the edges. There were tons of magazines but no music playing like in Dr Griffith's office. Here it was very quiet.

Pretty soon the nurse came back and said, 'This way, please.' We got up and followed her. She showed us into a smaller living room. It had a fireplace and everything. The ceiling must have been at least two storeys high. Daddy and Ma looked at each other and finally Daddy said, 'Well, he's supposed to be the best.'

I sat down in a big, soft green chair near the desk and Daddy and Ma sat on the little couch in the corner. In a few minutes there was a knock at the door and before we said anything a doctor came into the room. He looked a lot like the one in the movie I saw on Saturday. He sat down at the desk and said, 'I'm Dr Stewart.'

'But we're supposed to see Dr Kliner,' Ma told him.

'You will,' Dr Stewart said. 'I just want to get some information.' He opened a folder that was just like the one Dr Griffith carried around with him. Then he started asking questions. Daddy and Ma answered all of them. I didn't pay much attention until he said, 'Is there a history of scoliosis in the family?'

'Not in mine,' Ma said, looking over at Daddy, who cleared his throat and told Dr Stewart, 'I did have a cousin with a bad back. She was operated on for a slipped disc.'

'That wouldn't have anything to do with this,' Dr Stewart said.

'Then where did it come from?' Ma said, more to herself than to Dr Stewart.

'It's just one of those things,' Dr Stewart told her. 'It could just as likely be from your family as your husband's. We'll probably never know.'

'Hello, Deenie.' I hadn't heard Dr Kliner come in until he said that.

When I first looked at him I thought I might laugh. Because Dr Kliner looks exactly like Mr Clean, except he doesn't wear an earring. But his head is shiny bald – the whole thing – there's not one hair on his entire head.

He shook hands with Daddy and told him, 'I'm Henry Kliner.' I liked the way he said that. I've never heard a doctor call himself by his first name.

Dr Kliner leaned against the edge of the desk and looked at me. I could see his socks, which were white. The same kind we wear for gym. 'I've reviewed the X-rays,' he said. 'Now I want to have a look at Deenie.'

There were a lot of things going on I didn't get. How come Dr Kliner had my X-rays? And who was this Dr Stewart who stayed in the room and wrote things in the folder? I decided I'd better set things straight right away. 'I've made up my mind,' I said. 'I'm having an operation.'

'Deenie!' Ma said.

'I mean it. I am. I'm not scared or anything!'

Dr Kliner asked, 'Who's the doctor here, you or me?'

'You are,' I told him.

'Okay then . . . I want to examine you myself . . . go into the next room and get undressed . . . I'll be right in.'

I went into the next room and found one of those robes ready for me but this one was made of cloth instead of paper. It didn't fit any better than Dr Griffith's though. I was ready for Dr Kliner before he knocked at the door. 'Come in,' I called. Dr Stewart was with him.

'I'll bet you want me to bend over and touch my toes,' I said.

'That will do for a start,' Dr Kliner said.

We went through the same kind of examination that I had with Dr Griffith, only this time it didn't take as long. When he was done Dr Kliner told me I could get dressed and as soon as I came back to his office he said, 'There's no doubt . . . Deenie has a classic case of adolescent idiopathic scoliosis.'

'Why do you use that idiot–something word?' I asked.

Dr Kliner smiled at me. 'Sit down, Deenie.' He motioned towards the soft green chair closest to his desk. 'I think you should know about your condition. First of all we don't know exactly what causes it. That's why it's called idiopathic scoliosis. Idiopathic means without known cause.'

'Oh,' I said. So at least it isn't my fault and it doesn't have anything to do with being dumb.

'There are some things we do know,' Dr Kliner said. 'Scoliosis tends to run in families and it occurs mainly in girls. As a matter of fact, eighty–five per cent of all adolescent scoliosis occurs in girls. And the structural curve, which is what you have, usually progresses rapidly during the adolescent growth spurt. Do you understand?' Dr Kliner asked.

'Yes, I think so,' I told him. 'But do I have a C or an S spine?'

For some reason this made both Dr Kliner and Dr Stewart laugh a little. Dr Stewart has dimples, one on each side. He's cute for somebody his age.

Dr Kliner said, 'Your curve is more like an S than a C. And where have you been getting all this information anyway?'

'From my encyclopedia,' I told him.

'I see,' he said.

'I want to get fixed up as soon as I can so when do I get my operation?' I asked.

'I doubt that you'll need an operation,' Dr Kliner said.

Ma sighed, 'Thank God!'

'But how can you fix me up without an operation?'

Dr Kliner said, 'With a Milwaukee Brace.'

'I'd rather have an operation!'

'You think you would, Deenie. But let me tell you something about that. You'd spend months on your back recovering from it and there could be complications. In cases like yours we don't operate without trying the Milwaukee Brace first.'

'But I don't want to wear a brace. I just can't! There must be some other way.'

'Deenie,' Ma said. 'It'll only take a little while and then you'll be better.'

'How long?' I asked.

Dr Kliner didn't say anything for a minute. So I asked him again. 'How long will I have to wear it?'

'About four years,' he said.

'Four years!' me and Ma said at the same time.

'Until you've finished your growth spurt,' Dr Kliner told us. 'When you're about seventeen.'

'But she can't,' Ma said. 'You don't understand, Dr Kliner. Deenie's going to be a model. She can't wear a brace for four years.'

Dr Kliner raised his voice a little. 'I think you don't understand, Mrs Fenner. And it's important that you do.'

Daddy said, 'Look, Doctor . . . just fix Deenie up. That's all we really care about.'

'We will, Mr Fenner. We'll get that spine straightened out.' Dr Kliner went into a whole discussion about wearing the brace until my spine finishes growing and getting measured for it as soon as possible, maybe even this morning. And that scoliosis is more common than most people think. Dr Stewart left the room then but Dr Kliner sat at his desk answering Daddy's questions.

I thought, if I have to wear this Milwaukee Brace thing, no one is going to know about it. It will just be my secret. I'll be like Midge when she first got braces on her teeth. She said she wasn't going to open her mouth until the braces came off. For a while she even talked without opening her mouth, like a ventriloquist.

Dr Kliner stood up and walked towards a closet. I figured he was going to get his coat because with the air-conditioning on his office was kind of cold. But he didn't. Instead he reached in and came out with this weird-looking thing which he carried over to me.

'This is a Milwaukee Brace, Deenie,' he said. 'Of course yours will be made especially for you but this is just about the way it will look.'

At first I didn't believe him. I thought maybe it was some kind of joke. But then I knew it wasn't. Dr Kliner really meant it.

Dr Stewart came back into the room smiling. He said, 'Well, we're all set. You can go right over to the hospital and I'll meet you there. We'll make a mould of Deenie today and in a few weeks her brace should be ready.'

I wanted to scream, *Forget it . . . I'm never going to wear that thing. Everyone will know. Everyone!* But the words wouldn't come out.

Chapter 10

In the taxi, on the way to the hospital, Ma said, 'I don't see why Dr Kliner can't do it himself. That's what we're paying for, isn't it?'

'Dr Stewart makes all the moulds,' Daddy told her. 'I asked the nurse about it.'

At the hospital Daddy checked with some woman behind an information desk and then we went down a long hallway to a door marked PLASTER ROOM. 'This is it,' Daddy said, knocking. A nurse opened the door and Daddy told her I was Dennie Fenner and that Dr Stewart had called. The nurse smiled at me and said, 'We have five girls to mould today and you're number three.' Then she told Daddy and Ma they could wait outside and Dr Stewart would tell them when I was done.

Ma grabbed me, hugged me and cried a little. But Daddy said, 'Deenie's going to be just fine.'

I pulled away from Ma and buried my head in Daddy's jacket. I whispered, 'Don't go . . . I'm too scared.'

Daddy kissed the top of my head and said, 'There's nothing to be afraid of. I promise. Just do whatever Dr Stewart tells you and it will all be over soon.' He lifted my chin so I had to look at him. 'Okay?' he asked.

'Okay,' I said.

The nurse closed the door to the plaster room as soon as I stepped inside. I didn't even have a chance to look around before she pointed to a door and said, 'You can change in there. Take off all your clothes, including your shoes and put on both of these, one over the other.' She handed me two things that looked like very big socks.

The dressing room turned out to be a supply closet and I thought for sure somebody would open the door while I was naked so I tried to keep my back pressed against it the whole time I was getting changed. The things I had to wear were like body stockings. They fit very close and after I had gotten into the first one I looked down and noticed that you could see everything right through it. By the time I pulled the second one over the first you couldn't see as much and I was glad. Not that I have a lot to see but I didn't want Dr Stewart to see anything.

I adjusted the body stockings so they stretched from my neck down to my thighs. Just as I finished the nurse knocked on the door and called, 'Ready, Deenie?'

'I guess so,' I told her, opening the closet.

When I came out I saw that Dr Stewart was already there and so was some other guy dressed in a white coat.

Dr Stewart said, 'Deenie, I'd like you to meet

Dr Hubdu and Mrs Inverness, who will both be assisting me.'

Mrs Inverness was the nurse who gave me the body stockings and Dr Hubdu was from some other country. I could tell by his accent.

'Jump right up here, Deenie,' Mrs Inverness said.

I climbed on to an examining table.

'Now lie down . . . put your head back . . . just relax.'

Dr Stewart and Dr Hubdu were busy studying my X–ray, which was flashed on the same kind of screen I saw in Dr Griffith's office. They mentioned a lot of words like *lumbar* and *thoracic* and I didn't know what they were talking about.

I looked around the plaster room trying to figure out what was going to happen. The room wasn't very big. There was a counter with a sink, like in our kitchen. And right in the middle of the room was some kind of strange steel contraption with a rope hanging from a wheel on the ceiling.

In a minute Dr Stewart was measuring me again and calling out funny numbers and names to Dr Hubdu, who wrote everything down. The only words I got were *iliac crest* and *body firm*, whatever they meant.

'Okay, Deenie,' Mrs Inverness said. 'You can come off the table now.'

Dr Stewart sat down on a stool in front of the contraption with ropes. He motioned to me and I walked over to him. He held up some funny-looking thing and said, 'This is a head halter.' While he was talking he slipped it on me. It was made of two strips of white material and some string. One section of material fitted under my chin and felt like a scarf was tied there. The other part fitted around the back of my head and felt like I was wearing a head–band.

As soon as that was on me Dr Stewart attached a little wooden bar to the rope coming from the ceiling and somehow he hooked my head-halter to that. I was sure he was going to pull on the rope and leave me hanging in mid-air but just as I was about to ask him what was going on he said, 'We call this *hanging the patient* but you aren't really going to hang, because your feet won't leave the ground.'

I was glad to hear that.

Mrs Inverness said, 'Hold on to the bar above your head, Deenie. With both hands please.'

I reached up and grabbed hold of the bar.

'That's it,' Mrs Inverness said. 'Very good. You hold that the whole time.'

Dr Hubdu was behind me adjusting another wooden bar which came just under my backside. Dr Stewart told me to lean against it. I did but I guess I didn't do it the right way because Dr Hubdu said, 'Squat a little, please. Now just rest yourself against the bar as though you were sitting on it. That's better.'

Dr Stewart said, 'Lean forward a little. Good . . . just fine.'

Mrs Inverness ran a long piece of felt under my body stockings and down my back. Then Dr Stewart tied a strip of adhesive around my waist and attached each end to the wooden bar I was resting my rear end against.

After that he stood up and opened a small package of rubber gloves. I watched as he pulled them on. While he was doing that Mrs Inverness was busy at the sink in front of me. She was wetting strips of something. As soon as Dr Stewart sat on his stool again, Mrs Inverness handed him the wet strips and he began to wrap them around me. But after the first few he said, 'I'm not happy with this plaster, Nurse. Give me another roll please.' And he ripped off the strips.

As he waited for Mrs Inverness to wet some more he told me, 'When this dries it will become solid plaster. I have to wrap you tight in order to accentuate the hip line and chest. The brace will be made from this mould.'

I didn't say anything.

Mrs Inverness handed him some more strips and after he wrapped a couple of pieces around me he said, 'That's much better.' He wrapped me from my waist down to my hips and then from my waist up to my armpits. All this time Dr Hubdu stood behind me and I could feel his breath on my neck. 'Make sure her back is perfectly straight,' Dr Stewart told him.

'Yes sir,' Dr Hubdu answered. I got the feeling he was just learning about what was going on.

As Dr Stewart wrapped me up he smoothed the plaster with his hands. I didn't like it at all when he had to smooth out the strips across my chest.

'Head up, Deenie,' Dr Stewart said.

'Watch a point in front of you,' Mrs Inverness suggested.

Now both doctors were pressing on me, one at my back, the other at my front and I tried hard to stare at the handle of the cabinet over the sink.

'Stay just like that,' Dr Stewart said, as he moved his hands faster. 'We'll be finished in no time.'

'There are still some creases in the back, sir,' Dr Hubdu said.

'Smooth them out,' Dr Stewart said. 'We can't have any wrinkles.'

I thought about telling Dr Stewart that he was wrapping me too tight. That I really couldn't breathe any more. But that's when he said, 'Deenie's very cooperative, isn't she?'

And Dr Hubdu told him, 'She certainly is.'

I knew Daddy would be proud to hear that so I didn't say anything about feeling like a mummy.

A second later Dr Stewart ripped off his gloves

and said, 'That's the worst of it, Deenie. In a minute the mould will be hard and we'll cut you out of it.'

'It's very tight,' I said. 'And it's starting to feel hot too.'

'That's the chemical reaction. It's changing into hard plaster now.'

'I'm glad I don't have to wear anything like this mould,' I told him.

'Some scoliosis patients are still put into casts,' Dr Stewart said. 'But your brace will be a lot different. You won't mind it at all once you're used to it.'

Soon Mrs Inverness tapped me and said, 'It's hard, Doctor.'

Dr Stewart felt me himself. 'Good . . .' He whipped a ballpoint pen out of his pocket and drew little lines up and down my mould. Then he measured me again and Dr Hubdu wrote everything down, just like before. 'This will help the brace man,' Dr Stewart told me. 'Okay, Deenie . . . I'm going to cut it off you now. My saw makes a lot of noise but you won't feel a thing.'

His *saw*! I thought, he must be kidding!

But he wasn't. He had a regular power saw that made an awful noise and as he stood behind me running it along my back I was so scared that my teeth rattled. I tried hard not to move at all and prayed that Dr Stewart wouldn't miss with his saw and slice me in half.

At last he turned it off. 'Scissors please, Mrs Inverness.' A few seconds after that, he said, 'Spreaders . . .' I didn't know what he was doing back there but he kept pulling at me. Finally he said, 'There we go! Turn to the right, Deenie.'

I did and I was out of the plaster mould. Dr Stewart cut the tapes and took my head–halter off. I was free! That's when I looked down and discovered that I was only wearing one body stocking. Where was the other one? It must have stuck to the wet plaster and ripped right off. If they hadn't given me two of them I'd be naked! As it was I knew they could all see everything and I was so embarrassed I almost died. I tried covering my chest with my arms and bending over to hide my other half. I'm sure my face was purple and I felt like crying.

Mrs Inverness handed me a wet cloth and said, 'This will help wash the plaster off. You can go and change now.'

I ran for the supply closet. I didn't even realize the plaster had dripped on my legs and feet until then. But I didn't care. All I wanted was to get dressed and out of that room.

Chapter 11

That night I took my new nightie out of my bottom drawer and tried it on. I stood in front of the mirror and moved just enough to make it turn from pink to purple to lavender. Buddy Brader would never get to see it now and nobody would bring me pink roses either. I took the nightie off and packed it back in the Drummond's Department Store box.

I went to the phone and called Midge. Her line was busy so I tried Janet's number but that was busy too. They were probably talking to each other. I waited for a few minutes before I dialled Midge again. The phone rang three times, then Midge answered.

'Hi . . .' I said, 'it's me.'

'Hi Deenie . . . me and Janet were just talking about you. How'd it go today?'

'I'm not having an operation.' My voice was barely a whisper.

'You're not? How come?'

'I don't need one after all.'

'Well, that's great news! Isn't it?'

'I suppose.'

'You sound funny. Is anything wrong?'

'No . . . I'm fine. I just called to tell you since

I'm not having an operation I'll return the nightie. Listen . . . I have to run now . . . bye.' I hung up before Midge could say anything else.

I put the Drummond's box into a brown bag and carried it to school with me the next day. I knew it would be safe inside my locker. At lunch Janet said, 'We're really glad you don't need an operation, Deenie.'

I nodded.

'Were they wrong about your spine?' Midge asked.

'Not exactly.'

'But if it's crooked don't they have to do something?' Janet said.

'The doctors are trying to decide about that,' I told them.

'Me and Midge think you should keep the nightie anyway. Your birthday's in January so it can be a birthday present instead.'

'I really don't need it now,' I said. 'I'd rather return it . . . if you don't mind.'

They looked at each other.

'It's okay with us,' Midge said. 'We just didn't want you to think you *had* to return it.'

After school the three of us went to Drummond's. The same salesgirl was behind the counter. I handed her the box.

'She's not having her operation,' Janet told her.

'So she doesn't need the nightie,' Midge said.

'Well . . . aren't you lucky!' the salesgirl said to me, and she didn't even try to talk us into keeping the nightie or choosing something else in its place.

I tried to smile. I could tell that Janet and Midge knew something was wrong.

I stopped hanging around the cafeteria after lunch. I told Janet and Midge I had a lot of work to make up because I'd been absent so many times. As soon as I finished eating I went to the library where I sat with my books spread out on the table while I scribbled in my notebook or looked out the window.

One day, while I was sitting like that, somebody sneaked up from behind and covered my eyes with his hands.

'Guess who?' It was Buddy Brader. I'd know his voice anywhere.

'I give up,' I said.

He took his hands away and leaned up against the table. 'What're you doing in here, Deenie?'

'Make-up work,' I told him.

'I came in to watch the fish.' Mr Balfour, our librarian, keeps a big tank of tropical fish on the table in the corner and a lot of kids do wander into the library to watch them. 'You know something?' Buddy said, 'You didn't wave to me this morning.'

'I didn't?' Buddy waves to me every day when we pass each other in the hall, on the way to our first-period classes. 'I guess I didn't see you,' I told him.

'You turned away when I was walking by.'

'Well, I didn't mean to. I just have so many things on my mind.'

'Yeah?'

'I mean it . . . really.'

'Not that it matters . . . I only come in here to see the fish anyway.' He started to walk across the room. Then he stopped and turned for a minute. 'See you around,' he said. He must think I don't like him any more! I wish there was some way to let him know the truth.

All that week I kept hoping Dr Kliner would call to say everyone had made a terrible mistake. That there's nothing wrong with me after all and that I definitely don't have scoliosis. Every time the phone rang I jumped but it was never Dr Kliner. I touched my special place practically every night. It was the only way I could fall asleep and besides, it felt good.

We're starting a new programme in gym. Once a month we're going to have a discussion group with Mrs Rappoport. It sounds very interesting because Mrs Rappoport asked us each to write down a question and drop it into a box on her desk. The question could be about anything, she said, especially anything we need to know about sex.

She told us not to put our names on the paper. She doesn't want to know who's asking what. It's a good thing too, because I'd never have asked my question if I had to sign my name. I wrote:

Do normal people touch their bodies before they go to sleep and is it all right to do that?

On Tuesday, when we walked into the gym, Mrs Rappoport told us to sit in a circle so we could talk easily. The first questions she discussed were all about menstruation. But I already knew most everything from my booklet. After that she said, 'Okay, now I think we can move on to another subject. Here's an interesting question.' She read it to us. 'Do normal people touch their bodies before they go to sleep and is it all right to do that?'

I almost died! I glanced around, then smiled a little, because some of the other girls did, and hoped the expression on my face looked like I was trying to figure out who had asked such a thing.

Mrs Rappoport said, 'Can anyone help us with an answer?'

Susan Minton raised her hand.

'Yes, Susan . . .' Mrs Rappoport said.

'I wasn't the one who wrote the question but I've heard that boys who touch themselves too much go blind or get very bad pimples or their bodies can even grow deformed.'

'Has anyone else heard that?' Mrs Rappoport asked.

Five other girls raised their hands.

Could it possibly be true? I wondered. And if it was true about boys maybe it was about girls too. Maybe that's why my spine started growing crooked! Please God . . . don't let it be true, I prayed. I felt my face get hot and I had to go to the bathroom in the worst way but I didn't move a muscle. I hoped nobody could tell what I was thinking.

'Well . . .' Mrs Rappoport said, 'I can see you've got a lot of misinformation. Does anyone here know the word for stimulating our genitals? Because that's what we're talking about, you know.'

It got very quiet in the gym. Nobody said anything for a long time. Then one girl spoke. 'I think it's called masturbation.'

'That's right,' Mrs Rappoport told us. 'And it's not a word you should be afraid of. Let's all say it.'

'Masturbation,' we said together.

'Okay,' Mrs Rappoport said. 'Now that you've said it let me try to explain. First of all, it's normal and harmless to masturbate.'

'You mean for boys . . .' Susan Minton said.

'No, I mean for anyone . . . male or female,' Mrs Rappoport told us. 'The myths that some of you have heard aren't true. Masturbation can't make you insane or deformed or even give you acne.'

I wanted to take a deep breath when she said that but I didn't. I just gulped and looked at the floor.

'Does everybody masturbate?' Barbara Curtis asked.

'Not necessarily,' Mrs Rappoport said. 'But it's very common for girls as well as boys, beginning with adolescence.'

Any minute I thought Mrs Rappoport would ask us to raise our hands if we masturbate and I wasn't sure I'd be able to tell the truth. I never knew there was a name for what I do. I just thought it was my own special good feeling. Now I wonder if all my friends do it too?

But Mrs Rappoport didn't ask us to tell her if we did or we didn't masturbate and I was glad. It's a very private subject. I wouldn't want to talk about it in front of the class. She said the important thing to remember is that it is normal and that it can't hurt us. 'Nobody ever went crazy from masturbating but a lot of young people make themselves sick from worrying about it.'

I couldn't help thinking about Buddy. Can he get that special feeling too? I'd like to find out how much Buddy really knows about girls. I hardly know anything about boys. I think we should have discussions every week. They're more important than modern dance!

That afternoon, when I got home from school, there was a note from Ma, saying she was at the A&

P with Aunt Rae. I put my books down, poured myself a glass of milk and was just about to sneak a few chocolate cookies from Ma's secret hiding place, when the phone rang.

'Hello . . .' I said.

'Mrs Fenner?'

'No . . . she isn't in right now.'

'This is Dr Kliner's office calling . . .'

When I heard that my heart started to beat very fast. 'Can I take a message?' I asked then had to clear my throat.

'Deenie's Milwaukee Brace is ready and the doctor suggests an appointment on Friday at ten o'clock.'

'This Friday?'

'That's right. And the doctor also suggests a change of clothes for Deenie . . . a size or two larger than her regular things.'

'What for?' I asked.

'Because the brace takes up a certain amount of room and the girls can't get their regular clothes over it.'

'Oh.'

'Have Mrs Fenner call if she can't make it on Friday. I'll be here until six.'

'I'll tell her.'

'Thank you,' she sang and hung up, like she didn't even care about what she had just told me.

I didn't say anything to Ma about the phone call

when she got back from the market. I thought about not telling anyone. But I knew if we didn't show up on Friday Dr Kliner's office would call to find out what happened and then Daddy and Ma would know about the first phone call and that would make me a liar. So I told them during supper. It was already past six–thirty.

'Friday's fine with me,' Daddy said. 'I'll ask Joe to work that morning.'

I'd been chewing on the same piece of meat for a while but I couldn't swallow it so I held my napkin to my mouth and spat it out.

'What's wrong?' Ma asked.

'It was all fat,' I told her. I drank some water, then took a big breath and spoke very fast. 'I'm supposed to bring some other clothes to Dr Kliner's office because mine won't fit over the brace.' I looked at the food on my plate and moved some of it around with my fork.

'Don't worry about your clothes,' Ma said. 'You can get all new things . . . can't she, Frank?'

'Sure,' Daddy said. 'Never mind about that.'

'But my jeans are all broken in the way I like them!'

'So you'll break in new jeans,' Daddy said. 'As many as you want.'

'And I never even wore my two new skirts and sweaters. I was saving them for when it gets cold.' I could feel my throat tightening.

'Maybe we can take them back and get the next size,' Ma said.

'You already shortened the skirts,' I said.

'So we won't return them,' Daddy said. 'It's not important.'

'But it's a waste of money,' I told him.

'Never mind,' Daddy said again. 'All that matters is getting you well.'

'I am well!'

'You know what Daddy means,' Ma said.

Later, Helen came to my room carrying a navy skirt and a striped shirt. 'You can wear these tomorrow,' she said. 'They're bigger than your things and they'll probably look better on you anyway.' She put them down on my bed. They still had tags on them.

Chapter 12

The brace looks like the one Dr Kliner showed us three weeks ago. It's the ugliest thing I ever saw.

I'm going to take it off as soon as I get home. I swear, I won't wear it. And nobody can make me. Not ever! I felt like telling that to Dr Kliner but I didn't. I had to fight to keep from crying.

Just when I thought I was going to be okay Ma started. 'Oh, my God!' she cried. 'What did we ever do to deserve this?' She buried her face in a tissue and made sobbing noises that really got me sore. The louder she cried the madder I got until I shouted, 'Just stop it, Ma! Will you just stop it please!'

Dr Kliner said, 'You know, Mrs Fenner, you're making this very hard on your daughter.'

Ma opened the door and ran out of Dr Kliner's office.

Daddy hugged me and said, 'I'm proud of you, Deenie. You're stronger than your mother.'

I wanted to tell him I'm not. I hate just looking at the brace, never mind the thought of wearing it. But I was glad he thought I was strong so I kept pretending I really was.

'Why don't you see about your wife,' Dr Kliner

said to Daddy. 'I'd like a minute alone with Deenie anyway.'

Daddy said, 'Of course, Doctor,' and he left the room.

Dr Kliner pushed a button on his desk and told me, 'Miss Harrigan will be here in a minute. She's going to help you with your brace. But before she comes I want to tell you something. Your mother's attitude towards your condition is fairly common. Usually when the mother feels that way it rubs off on the patient. I can tell you have your father's attitude and I'm glad. Because wearing the brace can be as easy or difficult as you make it. Do you understand what I'm saying?'

I nodded.

'Before you leave we're going to give you a booklet about scoliosis which explains the exercises you'll have to do every day.'

'I didn't know I'd have to do exercises. I thought I wouldn't be able to do anything like that.'

'Just the opposite,' Dr Kliner said. 'There's nothing you *can't* do.'

'You mean I should take gym in school?' That would mean changing in the locker room where all the girls would be able to see my brace.

'Positively. Gym is very important. So is swimming. Can you swim?'

'Yes, but how do I swim with the brace on?'

'That's the one activity you do without the

brace. I'd like you to swim at least three days a week for half an hour at a time.'

There was a knock at the door and Dr Kliner called, 'Come in . . . Deenie I'd like you to meet Iris Harrigan.'

'Hello, Deenie,' Miss Harrigan was very tall and really pretty. She reminded me of that girl I sat next to at the modelling agency, the one who wanted to be in commercials. She picked up my brace and said, 'Let's go change.'

I stood up and followed her into the same room where Dr Kliner had examined me.

'You can get undressed in the bathroom if you want,' Miss Harrigan said. 'But take this in with you. It goes over your bra and pants.' She handed me a piece of material.

'It looks like a boy's undershirt,' I told her.

'It is a kind of undershirt. You wear it under your brace. It prevents most skin irritations.'

'I have to wear an undershirt? Like a baby?'

'Well, it's strictly for comfort.'

'Then I don't *have* to wear it?' I asked.

'It's not a *must*. But you'll feel more comfortable.'

'I don't care about being comfortable,' I said. 'I don't want to wear that thing!'

'Okay then,' Miss Harrigan said. 'Try it without.'

'I will.' I went into the bathroom and locked the

door. I took off my dress and folded it up. Then I unlocked the door and called, 'I'm ready . . .'

'Come on out,' Miss Harrigan said. She picked up the brace. 'I'm going to show you how to get into it now. The first time will be the hardest. After today it will be easier every time you do it.'

The brace is made mostly of metal but there are some white plastic parts too. Miss Harrigan explained that the reason the plastic is full of little holes is so the air can get through to my skin. There are two metal strips down the back of the brace and one down the front. But the worst thing is that the strips are attached to a metal collar.

Miss Harrigan helped me into the brace. 'It's too tight around my neck.' I tried to pull it away.

'It has to hold your neck in place,' Miss Harrigan said. 'The whole idea of the brace is to keep your spine in one position and your spine begins at the base of your neck.'

'It hurts!' I told her. 'Please take it off!'

'It doesn't hurt. There's nothing to hurt you at all. Let me adjust the straps for you.'

Miss Harrigan buckled and unbuckled the side straps until I told her I felt more comfortable. There were three more strips of metal on my brace that I didn't notice right away. Two are around my sides and one starts at the front of my neck, goes under my left arm, and winds up someplace in the back, near my head.

'It feels tight under my arms too,' I told her.

'You have to get used to that,' she said.

Besides the metal strips I had a whole section of white plastic around my middle and some kind of pad on part of my back.

'You'd be more comfortable if you'd wear the undershirt.'

'You said I didn't have to.'

'Why don't you take it home anyway, just in case you change your mind.'

'Maybe,' I told her. 'Right now I feel like I'm in a cage and no undershirt's going to change that! And suppose I grow? What happens then?'

'The brace is adjustable but if you outgrow it Dr Stewart will make another mould of you and you'll get a new brace.'

'I don't think I can live through this. I really don't!'

'I know it seems that way. But you will live through it. Lots of girls do.'

'That's easy for you to say. You don't have scoliosis.'

'That's true,' she said, like we were talking about the weather. 'But when you think of the alternatives, isn't wearing a brace better?'

'What do you mean? Better than an operation?'

'I mean better than growing up with a curved spine.'

'I don't know,' I said. 'I'm not sure about anything.'

Miss Harrigan walked over to a desk and opened the middle drawer. She took something out. 'I'm going to show you some pictures, Deenie. Then you can decide for yourself.'

She opened a booklet to some sketches of people with terrible-looking bodies, all crooked and bent over.

'Here's an illustration of a person with scoliosis, a side-to-side curve of the spine.'

'Like me?'

'Yes, except you'll never look that way. Aren't you glad?'

'I'd kill myself if I did.'

'No you wouldn't. But we don't have to argue about it because it's not going to happen.' She turned the page. There was a sketch of somebody who looked just like Old Lady Murray.

'I know someone like that!' I said.

'It's an illustration of kyphosis,' Miss Harrigan told me. 'A front-to-back curve of the spine.'

'Is that the same as hunchback?'

'Yes.'

It was hard to believe that I really and truly had something in common with Old Lady Murray.

When we left Dr Kliner's office I was wearing the brace with Helen's skirt and shirt over it. I was kind of scared that Ma would start crying again when she saw me. Instead she said, 'Well, that's not bad at all. You can hardly tell you're wearing it, Deenie.' I knew from the catch in her voice that she was just saying it and didn't mean a single word.

Daddy asked, 'How does it feel?'

'Like I'm in a cage,' I said.

As I was getting into the back seat of the car I whacked my head on the top of the door.

'Are you all right?' Ma asked.

'I don't know.'

'Let me see,' Daddy said, parting my hair. 'There's no blood,' he told us, as he rubbed my scalp.

'I guess I'm okay,' I said. 'I guess I just can't bend my head with this brace on.' As soon as I said that I started to cry. I cried the way I wanted to when I first saw the brace, loud and hard, until my throat hurt. Daddy didn't try to stop me. He just held me tight while he rocked back and forth, patting my head.

Chapter 13

The crying stopped as fast as it started. As soon as we got home I went up to my room and pulled off my clothes. I stood in front of my long mirror, inspecting the brace carefully from every angle. I was a disaster. I was as ugly as anything I'd ever seen. 'Damn you!' I shouted at my reflection. 'Damn you, crooked spine!'

I went to my desk and took out my scissors. Then I stood in front of the mirror again and hacked off one whole side of my hair. Right up to the ear. I watched as it fell to the floor. I'm crazy, I thought. I'm like the Deenie in the movie. When she went crazy the first thing she did was chop off her hair. I threw my scissors down, kicked the mirror and hurt my foot. That got me even more sore so I picked up the scissors and started cutting away at the rest of my hair. I cut and cut and cut until there was a big pile of hair on the floor and just a few loose strands hanging from my head. If I was going to be ugly I was going to be ugly all the way . . . as ugly as anybody'd ever been before . . . maybe even uglier.

Ma called from downstairs, 'Lunch Deenie . . .' and for some dumb reason that made me laugh because all of a sudden I was hungry. No matter how bad things are people still get hungry. That's a fact.

When I walked into the kitchen Ma was bending over the sink. She said, 'We're going shopping first thing tomorrow. Aunt Rae said she'll drive us downtown so you can get some new things for school.'

Daddy sat at the table and stared at me.

'What do you say to that, Deenie?' Ma asked, turning around. 'Oh my God! Deenie . . . what have you done to your hair?'

'I cut it.'

'Why . . . why did you do such a thing?'

'I felt like it.' I reached for my grilled cheese and tomato sandwich.

Ma put her hand across her mouth and shook her head.

I tried to eat my sandwich as if nothing was wrong. But I was used to bending over towards my food and with the brace on I couldn't bend at all. Not even my head. I couldn't really see my plate. I had to lift my sandwich straight up to my mouth. It was the same with my milk, which is probably why I spilled some of it down my front. Daddy jumped up to help me. He said, 'I think you'd be more comfortable if you pushed your chair away from the table. That way you can lean over and see your food.'

'I'm not hungry anyway!' I shouted, and in my

103

hurry to get away from the table, I knocked over the chair. I went up the stairs as fast as I could, slammed my bedroom door and tried to flop down on my bed. But I couldn't even flop any more. So I cursed. I said every bad word I knew. Every single one. I yelled them as loud as I could and then I screamed them again, spelling each out loud. I expected Ma to really punish me for that. She can't stand to hear those words. Once, when I was a little kid, she washed my mouth out with soap just for saying the F word. And in those days I didn't even know what it meant.

Later that afternoon I was in the bathroom. Even a stupid ordinary thing like sitting on the toilet wasn't the same for me now. The brace made everything different. And wouldn't you know it – that was when my period decided to come – of all the dumb times!

I called, 'Ma . . . Ma . . . I need help!'

Helen came to the bathroom door. I didn't know she was home from school already. 'Ma's not here,' she said.

'Where is she?'

'Daddy says she walked over to the A&P.'

'But she never walks anywhere.'

'I guess she didn't want to leave you home alone. Daddy's downstairs . . . do you want me to get him?'

'No.'

'Are you okay?'

'I just got my period and I can't get to the stuff.'

'I'll get it for you,' Helen said.

I sat on the toilet because I didn't know what else to do and in a minute Helen came in with the pads. I pulled my bathrobe tight around me. I didn't want her to see the brace yet.

She stood there looking at me.

I felt like a freak.

Finally she said, 'You cut your hair.'

I put my hand to my head to feel it. I'd forgotten about my hair. I thought Helen was looking at the brace.

She started to laugh then. 'It looks so funny,' she said.

'It just needs to be washed,' I told her. What right did she have to laugh at how I looked? 'Now could I please have the stuff?'

'Oh sure.' Helen handed it to me. 'Are you really going to wear it like that?'

'What?'

'Your hair.'

'Of course!'

'I could probably help straighten it out. It wouldn't be bad if I snipped off the strands that are hanging.'

'I like it this way!'

'Okay,' Helen said. 'Do you need any help with the pad?'

'No,' I told her. 'I can do it myself.'

'Okay,' Helen said again as she left.

But I found out I couldn't do it myself because I couldn't bend over to see what I was trying to do. Maybe if I'd been really experienced in wearing that stuff it would have been easier but this was only my second time. I dropped the pad by mistake and then had to figure out how to get it off the floor. Finally I did a knee bend, like Mrs Rappoport taught us in modern dance and I picked up the pad and started all over again.

When I came out of the bathroom Helen said, 'I thought you were planning to spend the night in there.'

'I had some trouble. It's not exactly the easiest thing to do when you're wearing a brace.'

'I'd have helped you.'

'I managed myself.'

'Well, cheer up,' Helen said. 'Janet and Midge are coming for supper and Ma's cooking your favourite . . . eggplant parmigiana.'

Chapter 14

I love eggplant parmigiana but I don't see why Ma had to invite Janet and Midge for supper. I'm not ready to face them yet. I need time to think and time to get used to the brace. I'm not even going to school on Monday. I'm almost sure Ma won't make me. Maybe next week I'll feel like seeing people but not now!

At five-thirty the doorbell rang, and in a minute Janet and Midge were knocking at my bedroom door, calling my name. I'd washed my hair and I was dressed in Helen's clothes again but I didn't let her snip off any extra strands of hair. When I opened my door Janet and Midge both said 'Hi,' in very loud voices, like they'd been practising.

Usually when we get together in my room we lounge on my bed or the floor but this time we just stood there and I could tell that Janet and Midge were being careful not to look directly at me.

Finally Midge asked, 'How do you feel?'

'Fine,' I told her. 'I'm not sick.'

'That's good.'

Then Janet said, 'We didn't know they'd have to cut off all your hair.'

'They didn't,' I said. 'I did it.'

'Yourself?' Janet asked.

'Yes.'

'How come?'

'Because I felt like it.'

'No kidding!' Midge said.

'That's a fact,' I told her.

'Well, it looks cool,' she said, glancing at Janet.

'Yeah, it's really different,' Janet said.

I turned and walked over to my bed. I sat down on the edge. 'Aren't you going to say anything about the brace?'

They looked at each other again.

'If you don't say something soon I think I'm going to scream!'

'But your mother told us not to talk about it,' Janet said.

'Oh . . . I should have known that was it!' I wish Ma would stop pretending. Does she think it's going to disappear if nobody says anything.

'Anyway,' Midge said, 'it's not so bad. An operation would be a lot worse.'

'You can hardly notice this,' Janet said.

I stood up. 'You're both lying!' I shouted. 'You're supposed to be my friends!'

'What do you want us to say?' Midge asked.

'The truth!'

They looked at each other.

'Well . . .' I said.

'Oh Deenie!' Janet said. 'We don't know what to

108

say or how to act or anything. We were going to make believe we didn't even notice.'

'And say that you looked swell, like always,' Midge said.

'But if you want to know the truth,' Janet said, 'it was a real shock, even though we knew the doctors would have to do something because you can't grow up with a crooked spine.'

'It's not called crooked spine. It's called scoliosis.' I reached for my notebook and opened it to the page I'd copied from my encyclopedia. 'You better read this,' I said, handing the notebook to Janet.

She and Midge sat on my bed and read it together. 'This is very interesting,' Midge told me.

'You don't know anything yet!' I said, and gave them a rundown on all the doctors I'd seen and how I had to be sawed out of my mould and everything. 'I'm thinking of becoming an orthopaedist myself.'

'But what about modelling?' Janet asked.

'I never wanted to be one anyway.'

'You didn't?'

'That's a fact.'

Ma called then. 'Deenie . . . supper . . .'

'Let's go,' I told them. 'I'm starving!'

As we headed down the stairs Janet said, 'You're really brave, Deenie. If I had to wear that thing I'd go to pieces. I'd never be able to live through it!'

That night when I got into bed I couldn't find a

comfortable position. No matter which way I turned the brace bothered me. I wanted to take it off but I knew if I did I'd only have to wear it longer. I was sure I'd never fall asleep again.

The next morning Aunt Rae picked us up in her car. When she saw me she cried which made Ma start in all over again. I was getting pretty tired of the whole thing. After all, I was the one in the brace, but the way they acted you'd have thought it was them.

We went downtown to Drummond's Department Store and I thought of my beautiful nightie. I wonder if anyone's bought it yet? We got off the elevator on the third floor – Junior Sportswear and Dresses. The saleslady started asking questions right away. 'What happened dear? Were you in an accident?'

Before I could say anything Aunt Rae told her, 'She's sick. She's got scoliosis.'

'I'm *not* sick,' I told Aunt Rae.

But Aunt Rae and the saleslady looked at each other as if to say I didn't know the truth and they did.

Meantime, Ma went through the racks pulling out things for me to try on. Size was a problem because the brace takes up a lot of room and everything I put on looked terrible. Besides, Ma and Aunt Rae were both talking non-stop about what kinds of clothes would hide the brace and pretty soon I did start to feel sick.

The saleslady kept taking things away and bringing them back in different sizes and after an hour of the same thing I couldn't stand it any more so I said, 'I don't want anything new. I like what I've got.'

'But what you've got doesn't fit, Deenie,' Ma said.

'So I'll wear Helen's old clothes. Just let's go home.'

'We're all trying to help you,' Ma said. 'But if you won't help yourself there isn't much we can do.'

'I just don't want to try any more on, that's all.'

Aunt Rae rushed back into the dressing room. 'I've found it,' she told me. 'The perfect dress.' Then, for no reason at all, she turned to the saleslady and said, 'Deenie's going to be a model, you know. Doesn't she have the most beautiful face?'

'Please Aunt Rae! I can't be a model now. You know that.'

'Of course you can. Where there's a will, there's a way. I'll think of something. Here . . . try this on.' She handed me the dress. 'The high neck will hide the brace.'

'I don't like it,' I said, looking at the white ruffles on the sleeves. 'It's too babyish.'

'Try it anyway,' Ma said.

'No!'

'Deenie, you're being stubborn!' Ma said.

'I'm old enough to choose my own things. Don't you think I know what I like by now?'

The saleslady was shaking her head and listening to every word. I wanted to yell at her — to tell her to mind her own business and get lost.

I got back into my things and told Ma, 'I'm going to the Ladies' Room.'

Aunt Rae followed me there. 'You know, Deenie, your mother would do anything for you. She's trying to make you feel better. It's not her fault this happened.'

'Well, it's not my fault either.'

Aunt Rae didn't answer that.

'It's not!' I said again. 'There isn't anything that anyone could have done about it. And if you don't believe me just ask the doctor!'

On Sunday night we were sitting around in the living room. Me and Ma were watching the end of 'The FBI' and Helen and Daddy were reading the papers. When the show was over I said, 'I'm not going to school tomorrow so can I stay up for the Sunday night movie?'

'Why aren't you going to school?' Ma asked.

'Because I'm not ready yet. I need more time to get used to wearing this thing.'

'I guess one more day won't matter,' Ma told me.

But Daddy said, 'Deenie's going to school, same as always.' He didn't even look up from the paper.

'But Frank,' Ma said, 'if she isn't ready . . .'

Daddy didn't let her finish. 'She isn't going to get any more ready sitting around the house feeling sorry for herself.'

'I'm not feeling sorry for myself!' I shouted, jumping to my feet.

Daddy looked up. 'Good . . . then there's no reason for you not to go to school.'

'Even if I'm sick?'

'You're not sick.'

'I think I'm coming down with something.'

'Frank,' Ma said, 'maybe it's the flu.'

'It's not the flu,' Daddy told her, 'and Deenie is going to school and that's that!'

'I never heard anything so mean!' I shouted.

'It's for your own good, Deenie.' Daddy stood up and reached for my hand but I pulled away and wouldn't let him touch me.

Chapter 15

On Monday I wore one of the smock shirts Ma bought for me on Saturday. Even though I told her I wasn't ever going to put on that stuff I was glad to have it.

'Hi,' Midge said when I got to the bus stop, 'I wasn't sure you'd be coming.'

'I had no choice,' I told her.

As soon as we got on the bus some lady asked me if I had been in a car accident. And later, when we were getting off at school, this boy I never saw before asked me what was wrong with my neck. I told them both the truth, that I have scoliosis and would have to wear a Milwaukee Brace for four years to straighten out my spine. Neither one paid much attention to what I was saying. If they weren't interested why did they ask me in the first place?

At school it was worse. Everybody wanted to know what was wrong including my formroom teacher who called me up to her desk and all the time I was explaining my condition to her she was patting me on the back.

Susan Minton practically glued herself to my desk and wouldn't leave until I told her the whole story. Then she said, 'Well, if I can do anything for you, anything at all, I'd be really happy to. I could carry your books around or help you up and down the stairs . . .'

I told her I didn't need any help and that I was just the same as before but I could see she didn't believe me. When the bell rang Miss Greenleaf told her to sit down at her own desk. Before she did Susan said, 'I think your haircut is terrific. I'm going to cut mine the same way,' which proved to me that Susan Minton is as stupid as I've always thought.

I waited in the formroom until everyone else had left for their first-period class because I didn't want to risk passing Buddy Brader in the hall. On Mondays and Wednesdays I have sewing first period, which is a terrible way to start the day. My sewing teacher, Miss Wabash, is about one hundred years old and very mean. She doesn't like me because I don't know anything about sewing. I wouldn't take it except the girls have no choice in seventh grade. We're required to have one year of sewing and another of cooking. At least the cooking teacher is nice. Janet has cooking this year and she says they have a lot of fun. When they clean up they always pretend they're doing a cleanser commercial for TV.

Midge is in my sewing class. We fooled around a lot the first week of school so Miss Wabash separated us. Now Midge's machine is right in front of

Miss Wabash's desk and mine is all the way across the room.

The minute I sat down at my sewing machine I remembered that we were supposed to buy our patterns and material over the weekend. As Miss Wabash called the roll each of us had to go up to her desk to show her what we had selected. It had to be either a skirt or a jumper. I hoped that Miss Wabash would understand why I forgot to get mine.

'Wilmadeene Fenner . . .' Miss Wabash called.

Practically all my teachers call me Deenie by now, but not Miss Wabash. She refuses because she says we have to get used to our given names. Midge found out that Miss Wabash's first name is Matilda. I'd love to call her that. It really suits her.

As I stood up I could feel everyone in the class staring at me. I went to Miss Wabash's desk and told her, 'I don't have my pattern or material yet.'

Miss Wabash didn't look at me. She seemed to be concentrating on something on her desk.

'What is the reason?' she asked.

'I was busy all weekend.'

'Doing what, may I ask?'

She still didn't look at me. I don't think she knew I was wearing my brace. Either that or she thought I always wore one.

I told her, 'I was busy getting my Milwaukee Brace.'

'Do you think that is a valid excuse?'

'I don't know,' I whispered.

'I do not think that is a valid excuse,' she said. 'Therefore I will have to give you a zero in this assignment. If you have your pattern and material on Wednesday morning I will erase the zero and give you a fifty. Do you understand, Wilmadeene?'

'Yes, Miss Wabash.'

'Good. Today you will practise seams on your muslin while the other girls cut their patterns. You may sit down now.'

I wanted to run out of the room. I looked at Midge and knew she was embarrassed for me. I sat down at my machine and sewed the most crooked seams I ever saw. More crooked than my spine because I couldn't bend over to see what I was doing.

Second period I have maths and right after Miss Varnicka put our problems on the board she came over to my desk to see if she could help. 'I think you'd be more comfortable standing at a lectern,' she said. 'If you'd like to give it a try I'll ask the custodian to bring one from the auditorium.'

'I don't think so,' I said. I could just picture myself standing in the corner at a lectern while everyone watched.

'Well,' Miss Varnicka said, 'then how about if you move your chair way back and lean forward with your body . . . that way you'd be able to see what you're doing.'

'I'll try,' I said. I pushed my chair way back, then leaned over my desk, and it worked! I could see what I was doing again. It wasn't exactly comfortable and the kid behind me had to move his desk too, but it was better than before and much much better than standing alone at a lectern.

All morning I kept wondering what Buddy Brader would think when he saw me. Once he told me that he likes girls with long hair and that mine was just perfect. I won't be able to shake it at him any more. Why didn't I think of that on Friday?

I was in the cafeteria, on the hot lunch line, when Buddy spotted me. He came right over and pushed in. The girl behind him yelled, 'Hey . . .' But Buddy just said, 'Hey yourself!' and he didn't move.

Then he looked at me and said, 'I heard all about your spine.'

'Who told you?'

'A lot of kids.'

'I guess practically everyone knows.'

'Yeah, I guess so. Now I know what you meant when you said you had a lot on your mind. Does it hurt?'

'No, it's just a little uncomfortable.'

'You can take that thing off sometimes, can't you?'

'I'm supposed to wear it all the time,' I told him. 'Except for swimming.'

'You even have to sleep in it?'

'Yes,' I kind of smiled then, to show how brave I am.

The lady behind the lunch counter called, 'Move along kids.'

'No gravy,' I told her, but she dumped a quart of it on my meat anyway.

Buddy said, 'No gravy,' too and she didn't pay any attention to him either. But as she went to put the gravy on his plate he moved it away and the gravy landed on the counter. 'That's what you should do,' Buddy told me. 'Otherwise you'll always wind up with it.'

The line was moving faster and I grabbed a roll and some Jell-O.

'I'm playing drums at the seventh-grade mixer,' Buddy said. 'You going?'

I was trying to dig out my lunch money to pay the cashier but I was having trouble holding my tray and getting into my purse at the same time. 'I don't know if I'm going,' I said to Buddy. I had to put my tray down so I could pay.

'You should go,' Buddy said. We walked across the cafeteria to where I always sit.

'Maybe,' I told him.

'You never heard me play drums.'

'I know,' I said.

'I'm good.'

'Well, maybe I will go . . . it all depends . . .'

'You should go.'

'Well, I probably will.' We were at my table and Midge was already there, peeling her eggs.

Buddy put his tray down and for a minute I wondered if he was going to eat with me instead of with his friends. He's never done that. But he didn't sit down. He reached over and put his hand on my head, kind of the way you'd pet a dog. 'You shouldn't have cut your hair,' he told me. 'It was nice long.'

I looked at Midge and she started choking on her eggs. She got up and ran to the fountain. 'I had to cut it,' I told Buddy, ' . . . because of the brace.'

'I didn't know that,' he said. 'It'll grow again, won't it?'

'Sure,' I said. 'I think hair grows almost an inch a month or something like that.'

'Listen,' Buddy said, 'I've got to eat my lunch now. Don't forget the mixer . . . I've got a solo and all.'

'I won't forget.'

He finally took his hand off my hair. I may never shampoo it again.

Chapter 16

That afternoon, when I got back to the formroom, Miss Greenleaf told me that Mrs Anderson, the vice-principal, wanted to see me after school. I couldn't imagine what I had done wrong but I knew it must have been something important to get called to the office.

I grabbed my books and sweater and went downstairs. There were three boys sitting on the bench outside Mrs Anderson's office and as I walked by they made noises at me. I tried to ignore them as I knocked on her door.

'Come in,' Mrs Anderson called.

I opened the door. Mrs Anderson was smiling. I've heard she always does, even when she's punishing kids. Her desk was in front of a big window but she sat with her back to it so she couldn't see the pigeon standing on the ledge. Ma says pigeons are dirty birds with lots of germs and I should stay away from them.

'Deenie Fenner?' Mrs Anderson asked.

'Yes,' I told her, holding my books tight against me.

'How did you do today?'

I didn't know exactly what she meant so I said, 'Fine, thank you.'

'No trouble?'

I wondered if Miss Wabash reported me? Should I tell Mrs Anderson it wasn't my fault I forgot the material?

Before I could make up my mind Mrs Anderson said, 'Now then, Deenie . . . the reason I sent for you . . .' She fumbled with a mess of papers on her desk and I was pretty sure she was looking for the note Miss Wabash must have sent to her office. 'Oh, yes . . . here it is,' Mrs Anderson said, holding up some kind of printed sheet that definitely wasn't a note from Miss Wabash. She waved it at me. 'How do you get to school, Deenie?'

'I ride the bus,' I told her.

'Take this form home and have your parents fill it out.' She handed it to me. 'You're eligible for the special bus now. It would be much more convenient and it's free.'

'You mean the bus that picks up the . . .' I started to say *the handicapped kids* but I couldn't — because all of a sudden there was a big lump in my throat. I had to look out the window so Mrs Anderson wouldn't notice. Another pigeon was on the ledge and both of them were walking back and forth looking at me.

'It's on your street every morning at ten after eight,' Mrs Anderson said. 'Deenie . . . Deenie . . . are you listening to me?'

'Yes,' I said in a voice that didn't sound like mine.

122

'Just have your parents fill in the form and return it to me.'

I barely managed to whisper, 'Okay,' before I turned and walked away.

I wanted to run off by myself but Janet and Midge were waiting for me outside. Janet was fooling around with Harvey Grabowsky. He kept grabbing her jacket and throwing it in the air and Janet was shrieking, 'Harvey . . . give it back!'

When Harvey saw me he asked, 'What happened to you?'

He *would* be the only one in school who didn't already know. 'I have scol . . .' I stopped in the middle. I didn't feel like explaining anything to anybody. Instead I looked straight at him and said, 'I jumped off the Empire State Building!' After I said it I felt better. I usually think up clever things to say when it's too late. From now on, when people ask me what's wrong, I'm going to give them answers like that. It's a lot smarter than telling the truth. Nobody even wants to hear the truth. 'I jumped right off the top!' I forced myself to laugh.

'Oh Deenie!' Janet said. 'Tell him the truth.'

'I just did.'

'Hey . . . that's a good story,' Harvey told me.

'Deenie . . .' Janet was annoyed now. She didn't like Harvey paying attention to me.

'Let's go,' I said. 'We'll miss our bus.'

'You go,' Janet said. 'I'm not ready yet.'

Me and Midge looked at each other, then walked away.

'He's not interested in her,' Midge said. 'He thinks she's a little kid.'

'She'll find out soon enough,' I told her.

We walked down the hill, past the church with all the statues, and around the corner. Old Lady Murray was fixing up her magazines as we got to the bus stop. I bought a roll of Life Savers from her. I stood closer than I ever had before. When she gave me my change I told her, 'I have scoliosis. That's why I'm wearing a brace.'

She didn't say anything.

'You have kyphosis, don't you?' She went back to stacking her magazines.

'I know you have kyphosis . . . that's what made your spine crooked.' Old Lady Murray didn't answer me. She started coughing. She had a terrible cough. Her face turned purple. I offered her a Life Saver but she brushed my hand away.

When she stopped coughing I said, 'Do you have any kids?'

'No.'

'Are you married?'

'No . . . I got nobody . . . no family at all.'

'But you have a mother and father . . . I mean, you did when you were small.'

'No.'

'But . . .' I almost called her *Old Lady Murray*. I

caught myself in time and instead I said, 'But *Miss* Murray . . . everybody has a mother and a father.'

'Not me,' she said.

'Then where did you come from?'

'The stork,' she said, and started to laugh.

'Deenie!' Midge called. 'Here comes our bus!'

I wanted to explain to Old Lady Murray that I wasn't fooling around with her. That I was really interested in her family. But Midge called me again and Old Lady Murray wouldn't stop laughing.

'Why did you have to start in with her?' Midge asked. 'Everybody knows she's crazy!'

'I never heard that,' I said.

'Well she is. Besides, she smells bad. Didn't you notice?'

'She smells like sauerkraut,' I said.

'Worse than that!'

'So does Harvey Grabowsky's breath.'

'What do I care about his breath?' Midge said. 'Tell it to Janet.'

'I think I will. Tomorrow.'

When I got home Ma and Aunt Rae were doing each other's hair. I went straight up to my room and tore the Special Bus Information sheet into tiny pieces. I wasn't taking any chances. Suppose Ma decided I should go to school on that bus? I'd absolutely die first!

On Tuesday morning Susan Minton was waiting for me outside the formroom. She had a haircut just like mine. There were even a few long strands hanging in the back.

'How do you like it?' she asked.

'Did you do it yourself?'

'No. My mother took me to her beauty parlour and I told Miss Lorraine exactly what to do.'

'If you'd done it yourself it would look better.'

'Really?'

'That's a fact.'

I thought Susan looked very funny and I almost told her so but that's when she said, 'We could be twins, Deenie. We really look alike now!'

'I suppose you wish you had a brace like mine too,' I said.

'I wouldn't mind,' Susan told me.

Miss Greenleaf shouted, 'Please sit down at your desks, girls. We're waiting for you!' I never got to tell Susan I think she's a mental case.

I spent most of the morning worrying about gym. I didn't want to change in front of all the girls. So right before lunch, on my way to the cafeteria, I stopped at the nurse's office. 'I don't think I should take gym this afternoon,' I told her. 'I've got my period.'

'How many days have you had it?' she asked.

'Since Friday.'

'Well, that's five days,' she said, counting on fingers. 'There shouldn't be any problem. Besides, exercise is the best thing for you. I never excuse girls from gym because of menstruation.'

'Oh.' I turned to leave.

'You're the Fenner girl, aren't you?' the nurse asked.

'Yes.'

'How are you managing with your brace?'

'Okay,' I told her.

'Good,' she said. 'Keep it up!'

I ran to the cafeteria, gobbled my lunch and hurried to the locker room.

Barbara Curtis is the only girl in my gym class who has a locker in my row. If I can change before she gets here I'll be safe, I thought. No one will have to see my brace. I took my sneakers out of the locker and set them on the bench, next to the gymsuit I'd been carrying with me. Ma fixed Helen's old one for me because mine doesn't fit over the brace. I kicked off my loafers and pushed them under the bench. Our gymsuits are one-piece so before I had to take off my skirt I was able to pull the gym suit up to my waist. Then I had no choice. I couldn't finish until I took off my shirt. My heart was thumping very loud. I sneaked a look down the row of lockers but nobody was there. So I stood facing the wall and unbuttoned my shirt. I got out of it as fast as I could, pulled on my gymsuit and zipped up the front. I made it! I thought.

But when I turned around there was Barbara

Curtis, standing in front of her locker, getting undressed. I'm sure she saw my brace, even though she had her back to me now. Her creeping crud was getting worse. It was all over her arms and legs . . . big red blotches and ugly hivey-looking things.

When Barbara turned around she caught me staring at her. I didn't say anything and neither did she. I sat down on the bench to put on my sneakers. I got my feet into them okay but I couldn't bend over to tie the laces.

'You want me to tie them?' Barbara asked.

'No,' I said.

'You'll trip over the laces.'

'I don't care.'

'I really don't mind tying them for you.'

'Oh . . . all right. If you want to.'

Barbara knelt in front of me and tied my shoes. I felt like the world's biggest jerk.

We walked into the gym together. When Mrs Rappoport saw me she didn't make a big thing out of my brace. She acted the same as always and I was glad. When she told us to choose partners me and Barbara looked at each other and grabbed hands.

Chapter 17

I've been wearing my brace two weeks and I've finally found a comfortable sleeping position, flat on my back. I never thought I'd be able to sleep that way but I guess if you're tired enough anything works. Besides, I've got a problem now. The stupid brace is making holes in my shirts. I've torn two new tops this week and Ma is really mad. She says we can't afford to keep buying things. I've told her over and over that it's not my fault. I don't even know how they get ripped. I think it has to do with the metal parts of the brace. But I've promised to be more careful anyway.

Daddy's joined the Y so I can go swimming. Midge belongs too and she's going to swim with me three days a week after school. The Y pool is heated which is nice. Dr Kliner told Daddy that I have to swim laps and not just fool around in the water. I wish I could swim like Midge because she's a regular fish. She can make it halfway across the pool without a breath. She's going to coach me so maybe we can make the Olympics together.

The best thing about swimming is getting out of my brace. I feel so free. But when the hour is up and I have to put it on again I could just cry! Sometimes I think I should throw it in the garbage and force the doctors to operate on me. But then I remember what Dr Kliner said about spending a long time in bed and I think of all the things I'd miss like the seventh-grade mixer, which is next Friday.

I wonder what would happen if I didn't wear the brace at all? Would I really turn out like Old Lady Murray? I wish there was a way I could find out for sure, without taking any chances.

Mrs Anderson sent for me again, this time in the morning.

'It's been two weeks and I haven't heard from you, Deenie.'

'You didn't say I had to come back.'

'But where's the form? I expected you to bring it in.'

'Oh that . . .' I looked out the window but no pigeons were on the ledge. I tried to think of what to say so Mrs Anderson wouldn't be suspicious. 'My parents threw that form away I guess.'

'Did you explain it to them?'

'Oh yes . . . but I told them I like riding the bus to school with my friends and they said that was fine with them so I suppose that's why they threw it away.'

'As long as they realize they could save money if you rode the special bus . . .'

'It's not that expensive. I get student discount tickets.' Could she tell I was lying?

'I've been talking to some of your teachers, Deenie . . .'

Is Miss Wabash after me again? I wondered.

'And they tell me you seem to be managing very well in spite of your handicap.'

How could she sit there and say such a thing to me! Did she honestly think I was handicapped? Is that what everybody thinks? Don't they know I'm going to be fine in four years – but Gena Courtney and those kids are *always* going to be the way they are now!

When I got home from school Ma and Aunt Rae were waiting for me at the front door. I hoped that didn't mean Mrs Anderson had called.

'We have good news for you, Deenie,' Aunt Rae said.

'What?' I asked, praying it wasn't about the special bus.

'Remember that modelling agency where we had to break the appointment . . .'

'Oh, not that again . . .'

'Listen to Aunt Rae,' Ma said.

'I told you I'd fix everything,' Aunt Rae said. 'I talked to the head of the agency himself, Deenie . . . and he told me that seventeen isn't too late to start out at all. So we can stop worrying. He'll be happy to see you when you're out of the brace.'

'But I don't even know if I want to be a model!'

'Of course you do!' Aunt Rae said. 'Isn't that what we've always planned?' She turned to Ma. 'Thelma . . . what's wrong with her?'

'She's just upset,' Ma told Aunt Rae. 'She's not used to the brace yet.'

'You wouldn't let her waste that face, would you?' Aunt Rae asked Ma.

'I'm not just a face!' I shouted. 'I'm a person too. Did either one of you ever think of that?' I ran past them and up to my room.

Ma yelled after me. 'Don't be ungrateful, Deenie! Aunt Rae was only trying to help.'

'Ha! I'll bet you'd both like to trade me in for some girl with a straight spine!' I shouted down-stairs. 'Then you wouldn't have to wait four years!' I slammed my door shut.

Chapter 18

Me and Midge have been discussing the seventh–grade mixer. She doesn't want to go and I know why. It's not just that she can't dance. It's mostly because she's a giant compared to the seventh–grade boys. I don't want to go either but on the other hand I don't want to miss it, especially because of Buddy Brader. I think Midge will go to the mixer with me if I promise that we'll just sit around and laugh but definitely not dance.

Janet keeps telling us that all seventh-grade boys are babies and it's a waste of time to go but I'm betting she'll change her mind at the last second. Steve Hildrick is the leader of the eighth–grade band and Janet knows it. Just because she's always hanging around Harvey Grabowsky doesn't mean she isn't interested in Steve too.

On Thursday afternoon Miss Greenleaf reminded us about the mixer. 'It's a good way to make new friends,' she said. 'After all, you come from four different elementary schools. Please make sure you wear clean clothes tomorrow . . . I want to be proud of my form.'

On Friday morning I knew I was right about Janet changing her mind. She wore a new outfit to school.

'How come you're all dressed up?' I asked her.

'I've decided to keep you and Midge company this afternoon,' she said.

'Gee, Janet . . . that's swell of you,' Midge said.

'I agree,' Janet told her. 'But I may have to pretend I don't know the two of you. You both look awful!'

Me and Midge decided to wear jeans to the mixer to prove we aren't really interested but I didn't think I looked *that* bad. My hair is beginning to grow. It covers my ears now and I had on a very nice turtleneck with my jeans. Turtlenecks do the best job of hiding my brace. Ma took two of my shirts back to the store yesterday and complained about the way they rip. The manager gave her new ones in their place. I'm sure he wouldn't have done that if he'd known about the brace. I'm glad he did though or I wouldn't have this purple top.

The rest of the day went so slow I thought it would never be three o'clock. I didn't see Buddy at all and I wondered if he was absent. If he was I wouldn't stay at the mixer. I'd tell Midge my stomach hurt and go home myself.

When the last bell finally rang and Miss Greenleaf dismissed us all the girls ran to the Girls' Room, just like the afternoon of cheerleading try-outs. Barbara Curtis was already in front of the mirror, brushing her hair. She made room for me. 'I like your turtleneck,' she said. 'It's a nice shade of purple.'

'Thanks.' I looked into the mirror and turned halfway around. You could still tell I was wearing the brace. I guess there's just no way to hide it.

Me and Barbara walked to the gym together. I told her I wasn't going to dance with anybody and she said she wasn't going to either. So I said she could sit with me and Midge and just watch. Barbara said that was fine with her.

Janet and Midge were waiting for me outside the gym. They didn't know Barbara so I introduced them.

'You're in my English class,' Barbara told Janet.

'I am?' Janet asked.

'Yes. You sit in the front row and I'm two rows behind.'

'No kidding! Who do you hang around with?'

'I'm new here,' Barbara said. 'We moved in over the summer.'

'I didn't know that,' I said. 'I thought you were from Lincoln.' That's an elementary school in another part of town.

'No, I'm from Chicago,' Barbara said. 'My father was transferred here.' She started scratching her arms. You could hardly see her creeping crud today because she was wearing long sleeves and high socks. Of course if you knew where to look, like me, you could always find it — on the back of her neck and in between her fingers.

'Do you have poison ivy?' Janet asked her.

'No, it's just my allergy,' Barbara said.

'You shouldn't scratch like that,' Midge told her. 'It'll only make it worse.'

'I can't help it,' Barbara said. 'When I get nervous I itch.'

'When I get nervous I have to go to the bathroom,' I said.

'I'd rather do that,' Barbara told me. 'You can always find a bathroom and be done with it. I'm never done!'

The four of us went into the gym together. I thought there would be decorations or something. But it looked just like always. A lot of kids were already there and most of the boys were racing around like idiots, which made me think Janet is right about them being a bunch of babies. Mr Delfone and Mrs Rappoport were trying to calm everybody down and get things organized. All in all it didn't seem like much of a mixer to me.

Then the eighth grade band arrived and everybody cheered. I was really happy to see that Buddy wasn't absent. It took three boys to carry in his whole drum set. I called, 'Hi Buddy. I'm here!'

He called back, 'Hi Deenie. I'm busy now.' He dusted off his drums while the boy with the guitar tightened his strings and Steve Hildrick played chords on the piano.

When they first started to play the band didn't sound very good and nobody danced. After a while they improved. Still, nobody danced, but the boys did stop playing touch football. Finally, Mr Delfone said we had to get up and dance. The band played the Alley Cat and most of the kids got on line, including Janet, but me and Barbara and Midge stayed where we were.

Janet's a very good dancer and she knows it so she practically led the Alley Cat. I noticed how she made sure she was dancing right up close to the band so Steve couldn't miss her, even if he wanted to. Sometimes I think Janet is getting to be a terrible flirt!

I love to dance. Last night I practised in front of my full-length mirror to see how I'd look dancing in my brace. And I found out I look terrible. So I'm not going to dance for the next four years, except secretly, to make sure I don't forget how.

After the Alley Cat they played the Mexican Hat Dance and the hora and I began to wish I hadn't come to the mixer. Watching other people have a good time isn't any fun at all. For the first time in my life I felt like a real outsider.

Then Mrs Rappoport told everyone to take partners and the band played the Gorilla. Danny Welker, who is this little freckle-faced kid who looks like he belongs in fourth grade, walked over to us. I've known him since kindergarten. He taught me every curse I know.

He said, 'Come on, Deenie. Let's go dance.'

'I don't feel like it,' I told him.

'Then what'd you come for?'

'To watch,' I said, looking away from Danny. I saw Janet dancing with this creepy guy from my maths class. His name is Peter and he has eyes like a rat and ears that stick out. Janet will dance with anybody! 'Why don't you go dance with Susan Minton,' I said to Danny.

'She's an ass,' he told me, grabbing my arm. 'Come on. You're wasting the music.'

I pulled away from him. 'I told you, Danny . . . I'm not dancing!'

He said all his curses at me, then looked at Barbara. 'I'll take you,' he said, pulling her up by the arms.

Barbara turned red and started scratching her neck. 'He's harmless,' I told her. 'Go dance.'

Danny practically dragged Barbara out to the middle of the floor and when he started dancing the Gorilla he really looked like one.

I turned to Midge, wondering if she was thinking that nobody's asked her to dance. Did she care or was she used to it by now? I couldn't tell from her face.

At four-thirty Buddy played his solo and everyone stopped dancing and gathered around his drums. I stood as close to him as I could but he played so loud I had to move back just a little or I might have gone deaf. You could tell how hard

Buddy was concentrating because he had his eyes closed and his hair was hanging in his face. He was even sweating. All of that made him look especially cute and I liked him better than ever. When he was done we all clapped for him and then the band took a break while Mrs Rappoport and Mr Delfone served pretzels and drinks.

I stood next to Buddy at the refreshment table. 'You were really good,' I said.

'I told you, didn't I?'

'I came just to hear you play!'

'I believe it,' Buddy said. 'I didn't see you dance once. Don't you know how?'

'Of course I do. I love to dance!'

'So how come you didn't? I saw Janet dancing the whole time.'

'She doesn't care who she dances with,' I told him. 'And I do.'

'Yeah?'

'That's a fact.'

'Would you have danced with me?'

'Well . . . sure.'

'Let's go dance then.'

'But there's no music.'

'Not in here,' Buddy said.

'Then where?'

'Come with me.'

He took my hand and led me to the door of the locker room but Buddy opened the door and

139

pulled me in so fast I had no time to do anything about it. It was very dark. 'Suppose somebody sees us?' I asked.

'Who cares?' Buddy put his arms around me and held me tight. 'I thought you said you know how to dance,' he said as he swayed back and forth.

'I do, but it's hard without the music,' I told him.

'Just make believe you hear it.'

'I'm trying,' I whispered, finding it hard to get the words out. I wanted to dance with Buddy. I wanted to in the worst way but all I could think of was my brace and I hated it more than ever. With all the people in the world why did I have to be born with a crooked spine! I pushed Buddy away from me.

'What's wrong?' he asked. 'You chicken?'

'No,' I said. 'Not exactly.'

'Then what, Deenie?' He got my back against the wall and put his arms out on either side of me so I couldn't get away. Then he put his face near mine. He's going to kiss me, I thought. He's going to kiss me and I don't know what to do.

Then he *was* kissing me but instead of enjoying it all I could picture was Mrs Rappoport catching us and sending me to Mrs Anderson's office. She'd call Ma, tell her I was making out in the locker room and I'd be in big trouble!

Soon Buddy came up for a breath. 'You *are* chicken,' he said. 'You don't kiss back.'

I didn't know I wasn't kissing him back. I never even thought about it.

'I'm not chicken,' I told him.

'That's good,' he said, moving one hand down from my shoulder to my chest. I know he was trying to feel me, same as Steve tried to feel Janet that day in the movies. I also knew that Buddy wasn't feeling anything but my brace, which only made everything worse, so I broke away from him and ran to the door.

'I have to go back to the gym,' I called. 'My friends are waiting.'

I opened the locker room door. Everyone was getting ready to leave. The mixer was over.

'Where were you?' Midge asked, when she saw me. 'I've looked everywhere! My mother's waiting for us outside.'

'I'm sorry,' I told her. I'd forgotten Mrs Otonis was going to pick us up at five o'clock. 'I didn't know it was so late. Where's Janet?' I asked.

'Already in the car.'

I looked around for Buddy. I wanted to say goodbye but I didn't see him anywhere. So I went outside with Midge and got into her mother's car. On the way home Mrs Otonis asked us all about the mixer and me and Janet told her it was really great but Midge didn't say anything at all.

Chapter 19

Barbara Curtis is a big liar! I knew it on Saturday morning as soon as I woke up. Her creeping crud *is* catching! I've got it on my back and chest. It itched all night and spoiled my dream about Buddy.

I called down to the kitchen, 'Ma . . . come up here quick! I've got something all over me!'

'What is it?' Ma asked, rushing up the stairs.

'Look . . .' I showed her my creeping crud.

She inspected it. 'I'll call Dr Moravia,' she said.

I followed her to the phone and listened as she explained it to him.

When Ma hung up I asked, 'What did he say?'

'That I should take you to Dr Nelson.'

'Who's he?'

'A dermatologist.'

'What's that?'

'A doctor who specializes in skin conditions.'

'I don't want to see another doctor! Can't we just use calamine or something?'

'No, we have to take care of it. You don't want it to spread to your face do you?'

I thought about Barbara. She didn't have the creeping crud on her face but it *was* on her neck. 'No,' I told Ma. 'I don't want it on my face.'

'All right then. Get dressed. Dr Moravia said he'll make an appointment for us to see Dr Nelson.'

At noon Aunt Rae came over and drove us downtown to Dr Nelson's office. His nurse told me to get undressed. She handed me a sheet to wrap around myself. Ma stayed in the room with me the whole time.

When Dr Nelson came in I decided right away that I didn't like him. He wasn't friendly like Dr Kliner. He didn't even say hello to me. He just turned on a bright light and held a magnifying glass to my creeping crud.

'I caught it from Barbara Curtis, this girl in my gym class,' I told him.

'I don't think so,' he said.

'She's the only one I know who's got it.'

'What you have isn't contagious.'

'It's not?'

Dr Nelson didn't answer me. He touched my rash and looked at it some more. Then he sat down at his desk and wrote out some prescriptions which he handed to Ma.

'If it's not catching then what is it?' I asked.

'An irritation from your brace. You shouldn't wear it next to your skin. You need a soft shirt under it.'

'Not one of those things I saw in Dr Kliner's office?' I said.

'I don't know what you saw but you'll have to

wear an undershirt to protect your skin from now on.'

'Oh no! I'm not wearing any undershirt!'

'Deenie . . .' Ma said. 'You'll do whatever the doctor tells you.'

'And that means a soft undershirt,' Dr Nelson said again. 'I'm also prescribing a cortisone cream to rub in three times a day and a solution to put into your bath water. Soak for half an hour a day until the rash clears up. Call me if it doesn't improve in a week,' he told Ma as he stood up.

As soon as he left the room Ma said, 'Get dressed, Deenie, and we'll stop by the drugstore on our way home.'

An undershirt! I thought as I got into my clothes. How can I go to school in an undershirt?

That night Ma ran my tub and dumped in one package of the powder Dr Nelson prescribed. 'I'm setting the oven so I know when half an hour's up,' Ma said. 'I'll call you. Soak until then.'

I got out of my brace and into the tub. At first I was bored just lying there. Usually I take showers and get in and out as fast as possible. But the hot water was very relaxing and soon I began to enjoy it. I reached down and touched my special place with the washcloth. I rubbed and rubbed until I got that good feeling.

There are still a lot of things I don't understand

about sex. I think Helen has a book somewhere in her room. I'm going to look for it.

When Ma called that my time was up I got out of the tub, dried off and put on the undershirt before my brace. I think what I'll do is wear my bra under it. I'm certainly not going to school without a bra.

I tiptoed into Helen's room. She's never home anymore. And when she is home she's always locked up in her room. I think something's wrong with her. She got two B's on her report card and that's never happened before. Ma was plenty sore too!

I opened Helen's desk drawers one by one. I didn't see the book I was looking for but I did find a piece of notebook paper that said:

Mrs Joseph Roscow
Helen and Joe Roscow
Joseph and Helen Roscow
Helen Marie Roscow
Helen Fenner Roscow
Mr and Mrs Joseph P. Roscow

At first I didn't know what all those names meant. Then it hit me. Helen was writing about Joe, from Daddy's gas station, and herself. Helen was in love!

Not long after that Ma found out about Helen too. Because one night after supper Daddy went back to the station to do his books and Helen was there with Joe, while she was supposed to be studying at Myra Woodruff's house.

I don't know exactly what happened but Daddy drove Helen home and she wasn't allowed out at night for the next two weeks, except to do her baby-sitting.

Helen cried a lot those two weeks. I heard her every night.

Then one afternoon Helen came home and started screaming at Ma. 'How could you? How could you be so mean?'

'It's not what you think,' Ma told her.

I wondered what was going on? I thought, maybe Helen and Joe want to get married and Ma won't let them.

'You *made* Daddy fire him just because we liked each other!' Helen shouted.

'That's not so,' Ma told Helen. 'Daddy had to let him go because we need the extra money. You can ask him yourself.'

'You're lying!' Helen yelled. 'You did it because you don't want us together. Admit it . . . admit it, why don't you? You don't need the money.'

'Yes we do!' Ma said. 'I'll discuss it with you when you calm down.'

'I'm calm now,' Helen hollered.

Ma raised her voice too and I felt very uncomfortable. I wanted to leave the room but I didn't want to miss the argument. So I sat in my chair and listened.

'We have doctors' bills to pay,' Ma shouted. 'And we're going to have more of them. Until I can find some work Daddy's going to manage without help at the station.'

Doctors' bills, I thought. Ma must be talking about *my* doctors! I'll bet my brace cost a fortune. I didn't think of that before. I'm the reason Daddy had to fire Joe. Helen is going to hate me!

'You didn't approve of him anyway,' Helen told Ma.

'I don't want you throwing away your life,' Ma said.

'I wasn't throwing away my life! I just wanted to be with him. Is that so wrong? I'm sixteen, Ma! I'm not a baby!'

'He wasn't right for you,' Ma said.

'How do you know? Who are you to say what's right for me? It wouldn't bother you if a boy liked Deenie would it?'

Why did she say that? I wondered.

'That's different,' Ma said.

'What's different about it?' Helen asked. 'I'm human too.'

'God gave you a special brain,' Ma told her. 'And he wouldn't have done that if he hadn't intended for you to put it to good use.'

147

She's telling Helen the same thing she told me about my face!

'Oh Ma . . . you're impossible! God didn't give me a special brain. You made that up. And you almost convinced me, Ma . . . you almost did.' Helen was really crying now. Tears ran down her face and everything but she didn't stop. She said, 'I used to tell myself it didn't matter if I wasn't pretty like Deenie because I have a special brain and Deenie's is just ordinary . . . but that didn't help, Ma . . . it didn't help at all . . . because it's not true! None of it's true . . . don't you see . . . you can't make us be what you want . . .' Helen was sobbing so loud she couldn't talk anymore.

I didn't know what to do. I was hoping Helen and Ma had forgotten I was in the room. I wished I could vanish. I never knew Helen thought about me being pretty. I always thought it was just the opposite . . . that she was better than *me* because she was so smart. I feel funny knowing about Helen.

'If you think I'm going to sit by and watch you waste your life on a stupid boy with dirty finger-nails you have a lot to learn, Helen Fenner!' Ma said.

'He's not stupid!' Helen cried. 'He's going to be a Forest Ranger and he writes poems . . . did you know that? Do you know anything about him?'

Ma's not being fair, I thought. Joe does write

148

poems. I know because I found one inside Helen's maths book last Wednesday. I couldn't tell that to Ma though. Then Helen would know I'd been snooping, so instead I said, 'Everybody gets dirty fingernails from working in a gas station . . . even Daddy!'

'Be quiet, Deenie!' Ma yelled. 'This has nothing to do with you.'

'It does too! You just said Daddy fired Joe because of doctors' bills and I'm the one who's always seeing doctors!'

Helen turned around and looked at me. Then she did the craziest thing. She ran to me and hugged me and cried into my shoulder. 'It's not your fault, Deenie . . . don't let them make you believe that . . . it's really not your fault.'

I started crying too. Helen doesn't hate me, I thought. She should, but she doesn't. We both cried so hard our noses ran but neither one of us let go of the other to get a tissue. And right through it all Ma kept talking. 'I wanted better for you,' she said. 'Better than what I had myself. That's what I've always planned for my girls . . . is that so wrong?'

149

Chapter 20

I finally told Barbara Curtis about my undershirt. I got tired of rushing to the Girls' Room every time I had gym. And that's what I've been doing — taking off my undershirt and stuffing it in my bag.

As soon as I told Barbara I felt better. She said one time the rash between her fingers was so bad she had to wear white socks on her hands at night, to keep from scratching in her sleep. She asked me what kind of cream I'm using and I described it to her. She said it sounds a lot like hers. I think my rash is getting better because it doesn't itch anymore.

I'm glad Barbara's not a liar after all. She's a nice kid. I think I must have been really weird to not like her just because of her creeping crud. Janet and Midge like her too. Janet invited her to a party she's having in two weeks. She's also invited Harvey Grabowsky which is the dumbest thing I've ever heard. I know he isn't going to come.

I dropped another question into Mrs Rappoport's box. I wrote:

What does it feel like to have sexual intercourse?

The other night, when I'd finished my exercises, I

went to Helen's room and asked if I could borrow her sex book.

'I lent it to Myra,' she said. 'You can read it when she gives it back.'

'But I need it now,' I said.

'What for?'

'Because . . .'

'You have a question?'

I nodded.

'Maybe I can help you.'

'I have a lot of questions,' I told her.

'Go on . . .'

'Well . . .'

'If you're going to be shy about it I can't help you.'

'All right,' I said. 'What does it feel like to have sexual intercourse?' As soon as I said it I was sorry because Helen turned colours. 'You told *me* not to be shy!' I said.

'I don't know the answer.'

'Oh, come on, Helen.'

'I really don't know,' Helen said. 'And now that Joe's gone I'll probably never find out!'

Joe left town without telling Helen. I think that was really rotten of him. Maybe he didn't love her after all. I hope Helen finds somebody else to love soon, because I can see how lonely she is without Joe. I also hope Mrs Rappoport can help me with my questions and that Myra hurries with the sex book.

I got a letter from Dr Kliner inviting me to a scoliosis clinic at his office, where all of his patients get together to talk about wearing their braces. I think I'll ask the other girls how they sit at their desks and if they get rashes too and if they all sleep flat on their backs and rip their clothes and worry about people looking at them wherever they go? And I'm going to tell them how I answer people who ask me what's wrong. I'll bet I'm the only one who's ever said, 'I jumped off the Empire State Building!' The most important thing I have to find out is how smart you have to be to become an orthopaedist because I've been thinking I might really like to be one.

This afternoon, on my way to French, I didn't look away when I passed the Special Class. I saw Gena Courtney working at the blackboard. I wonder if she thinks of herself as a handicapped person or just a regular girl, like me.

Chapter 21

I'm not going to wear the brace to Janet's party. It can't hurt to take it off for a few hours. I do it three times a week when I go swimming, and I want Buddy Brader to see me without it. I want him to hold me the way he did in the locker room, without feeling all that metal.

I got dressed in one of the outfits I bought to start junior high — a skirt and sweater that doesn't fit over the brace. I wasn't sure how Daddy and Ma would take it but I had the feeling they'd let me go because I haven't been complaining about the brace and I haven't asked to skip school again.

I went downstairs. 'I'm ready to go to Janet's,' I told Daddy.

He looked at me. 'Where's your brace?'

'I'll put it on as soon as I come home.'

'You can't go without it.'

'Please Daddy . . . this is very important to me.'

'No,' he said. 'If I let you go without it now you'll want to leave it off every time you're going somewhere special.'

'No, I won't. I promise . . . just this once!'

'Go upstairs and change.'

'But Daddy . . .'

153

'Oh, let her go, Frank,' Ma said. 'She looks so pretty.'

Daddy slammed the book he was reading and shouted at Ma. 'We've been through this before, Thelma.' Then he turned to me and I thought he was going to yell but when he spoke his voice was back to normal. 'The day I found out about your brace I promised myself I'd be firm,' he said. 'That's why I made you go to school when you wanted to stay home. And now I'm telling you . . . no matter how much it hurts . . . you wear the brace or you don't go.'

'But Daddy . . .'

'I know . . . I know,' he said. 'It's hard for me too, Deenie.'

I ran up to my room and kicked the door shut. My father wasn't going to change his mind – even if I screamed and cried he wasn't going to change it. I knew that. I didn't want to miss Janet's party. I didn't want to miss a lot of things that would be happening in the next four years. But just tonight I wanted to be like everyone else.

Suppose I wore the brace to the party and as soon as I got there I changed? That way Daddy wouldn't know anything because my friends won't tell on me. And I'll never do it again. I swear this is the first and last time!

I changed into the brace and my regular clothes

but I packed the outfit I'd been wearing into a shopping bag. Then I went downstairs.

Daddy drove me to Janet's house and when we got there he leaned over and kissed the top of my head. 'I'm glad you changed your mind, Deenie. I knew you wouldn't let me down.'

I felt bad about fooling him. I grabbed my shopping bag and opened the car door.

'Have a good time,' Daddy said.

'I will,' I told him, as I got out of the car.

The front door of Janet's house was open and as I walked in I could hear all the noise coming from her basement. I thought about going straight up to Janet's room to change before anybody saw me. Then I thought about my father and how he trusts me. I've never really lied to him and I don't think he's ever lied to me. I put my shopping bag down in the corner of the living room and went downstairs. Maybe I'd change later.

Janet has this great basement with flowers painted all over the concrete floor and posters decorating every pole. Midge and Barbara were already there. So was Buddy Brader.

'Hey, Deenie,' he said, when he saw me. 'What took you so long? I thought you weren't coming.'

'Well, I'm here now,' I said.

Mr Kayser served us a ton of food. There was a dish with rows and rows of turkey and roast beef. I guess he gets it cheap because he's a butcher. Janet said she promised her mother we'd play nice, decent games like charades even though none of us wanted to. Naturally Harvey Grabowsky didn't show up. I guess Janet finally realized he wasn't going to and she settled for Steve Hildrick instead. When she put on the record player they started dancing and I saw her press up against him.

Later Buddy grabbed my hand and led me into the part of the basement where Janet's mother does the laundry. It was dark and kind of damp in there and it smelled like Clorox. Buddy said, 'Couldn't you take off your brace for a little while?'

I thought about the shopping bag I'd left upstairs. 'No,' I told Buddy. 'I have to wear it all the time.'

'Oh well . . .' Buddy said. This time when he kissed me I concentrated on kissing him back. I hoped I was doing it right.

Daddy called for me at eleven-thirty and as I got into the car he asked what was in the shopping bag. I told him, 'Something I thought I might need for the party . . . that I didn't need after all.'

Judy Blume talks about writing *Deenie*

I met a lively fourteen-year-old with scoliosis. She seemed to be adjusting well to her condition and her brace, but her mother was in tears over the situation. The basic idea for the book came from that meeting. But I invented the characters and the family. I set the book in the town where I grew up – Elizabeth, New Jersey – and sent Deenie and her friends to my junior high school. I think of the story as one about parental expectations. Deenie's mother says: *Deenie's the beauty, Helen's the brain.* What happens when a parent pigeonholes her children that way?

Since I wrote the book, new ways of treating scoliosis have been developed, though some patients still wear the Milwaukee Brace. If you need up-to-date info, try www.iscoliosis.com or www.scoliosislife.net. You can also try the Scoliosis Association, Inc., an international information and support organization: www.scoliosis-assoc.org

Last week my parents had another big fight.
Val says people get divorced all the time.
But there must be a way I can stop this
happening to our family . . .

When Karen's parents announce they're getting divorced,
it feels like her heart is about to break and she scores the
day with a big fat D-. So what if other people's parents
break up – Karen is determined to keep her family
together, whatever it takes. But trying to force two people
to love each other again isn't easy and Karen begins to
realize that maybe it's not the end of the world . . .

Turn the page to read an extract

Chapter 1

I don't think I'll ever get married. Why should I? All it does is make you miserable. Just look at Mrs Singer. Last year she was Miss Pace and everybody loved her. I said I'd absolutely die if I didn't get her for sixth grade. But I did – and what happened? She got married over the summer and now she's a witch!

Then there are my parents. They're always fighting. My father was late for dinner tonight and when he got home we were already at the table. Daddy said hello to me and Jeff. Then he turned to Mom. 'Couldn't you have waited?' he asked her. 'You knew I was coming home for dinner.'

'Why didn't you call to say you'd be late?' Mom asked.

'It's only twenty after six. I got hung up in traffic.'

'How was I supposed to know that?' Mom asked.

'Never mind!' My father sat down and helped himself to a slice of meat loaf and some Spanish rice. He took a few mouthfuls before he said, 'This rice is cold.'

'It was hot at six o'clock,' Mom told him.

Me and Jeff kept on eating without saying a

3

word. You could feel what was going on between my parents. I wasn't hungry any more.

Then Daddy asked, 'Where's Amy?'

'In the den,' Mom said.

'Did she eat?'

Mom didn't answer.

'I said did she eat her supper?'

'Of course she did,' Mom snapped. 'What do you think I do — starve her when you're not around?'

My father pushed his plate away and called, 'Amy . . . Amy . . .'

Amy is six. When she doesn't like what we're having for dinner she eats a bowl of cereal instead. Then she races into the den to see her favourite TV show. But when Daddy called her she ran back to the kitchen. She gave him a kiss and said, 'Hi, Daddy.'

'How's my girl?'

'Fine.'

'Sit down at the table and drink your milk,' he said.

'First a riddle,' Amy told him.

'Okay, but just one.'

Amy is driving us crazy with her riddles. Ever since she started first grade it's been one riddle after another. And you can't tell her you already know the answer because she doesn't care. She'll keep asking anyway.

4

'Why did the man put Band-Aids in his refrigerator?' Amy asked.

'I give up,' my father said.

'Because it had cold cuts!' Amy laughed at her joke. She was the only one who did. 'You get it now? *Cold cuts*. The refrigerator had cold cuts! Like bologna . . . get it?'

'I get it,' Daddy said. 'That's a very good riddle. Now sit down and drink your milk.'

As Amy sat down she accidentally shook the table and her milk spilled all over the place. Mom jumped up to get the sponge.

'Don't be mad, Mommy. It was an accident,' Amy said.

'Who's mad?' my mother shouted. She mopped up the mess. Then she threw the sponge across the kitchen. It landed on the counter, next to the sink. 'Who's mad?' she hollered again as she ran out of the room and down the hall. I heard a door slam.

My mother's temper is getting worse. Last week she baked a cake. When she served it my father said, 'That's not mocha icing, is it?' And my mother told him, 'Yes, it is.' So Daddy said, 'You know I can't stand mocha. Why didn't you make chocolate?' And Mom said, 'Because I'm sick of chocolate, that's why!'

I love dessert and by then my mouth was really watering. I wished they would hurry and finish talking about it so I could start eating.

But my father said, 'I'll have to scrape off the icing.'

Mom looked right at Daddy and told him, 'Don't do me any favours!' Then she picked up that beautiful cake, held it high over her head and dropped it. It smashed at my father's feet. The plate broke into a million pieces and the chips flew all around. It was one of our ordinary kitchen plates. I'll bet if it was an antique, my mother never would have dropped it like that.

Later, when nobody was looking, I snitched a piece of cake off the floor. Even though it had fallen apart it was still delicious.

But that was last week. Tonight Mom didn't throw anything but the sponge. As she ran out of the kitchen my father cursed, crumpled up his napkin and got up from the table. Jeff pushed his chair away too, but my father hollered, 'You stay right where you are and finish your dinner!' He grabbed his coat and went out the back door. In a minute I heard the garage door open and the car start.

'You really picked a great time to dump your milk,' Jeff told Amy. He is fourteen and sometimes very moody.

'I didn't do it on purpose,' Amy said. 'You know it was an accident.'

'Well, I hope you're happy,' he told her. 'Because

the whole rotten night's ruined for all of us now!'
He cursed like my father and Amy started to cry.

'I'm going to my room,' she told us. 'Nobody
loves me any more!'

Jeff was the next one to walk out of the kitchen,
leaving me there alone. I knew where he was
going. To his private hideaway. It's on the third
floor and it used to be the spare room. The ceiling
is low on one side and the windows are small and
up high. I don't see why anybody would want to
sleep in there if he didn't have to.

Jeff spent a lot of time decorating it. There's a
big sign on the door that says *Jeff's Hideaway/All
Who Enter Do So at Their Own Risk*. Then there's a
purple light hanging from the ceiling and a million
posters all over the walls. It's very messy too. In
the fall we had to have the exterminator because
of Jeff. He took so many cookies and crackers and
cans of soda up there we got bugs. My father was
really sore! Jeff doesn't throw his garbage under
the bed any more. And he's not supposed to drink
soda anyway. It's bad for his zits. My mother calls
them pimples and says he's lucky that he's only got
one or two.

His zits don't stop the girls from calling though.
They call all the time. My father has threatened to
limit Jeff's phone conversations to two minutes.
Jeff doesn't care. There's only one girl he wants to
talk to anyway. That's Mary Louise Rumberger.

She's in his formroom. I've only seen her once. She has very nice hair and she smells like Noxzema.

I know what Jeff does up in his room. He lifts weights. Isn't that the dumbest thing? He wants to be on the wrestling team next year. My mother's worried sick because she's afraid he'll get hurt. I wonder if maybe Mary Louise Rumberger likes big muscles?

Chapter 2

The house was very quiet. I was still sitting at the dinner table, making little designs on my plate with the Spanish rice. I thought about clearing away the dishes and even stacking them in the dishwasher. But why should I? I didn't start the fight. It wasn't my fault dinner was ruined. I wondered if my mother had something special planned for dessert. I wasn't about to ask her though. She was probably locked up in her bathroom.

I went to the pantry and took down a box of chocolate-chip cookies. On my way upstairs I scooped up Mew, who was sitting on her favourite chair in the living room.

She is supposed to be the family cat but she loves me best. Probably because she knows I love *her* more than anything in the world. From far away it looks as if Mew's coat is dark grey, but when you get up close you can see that she's really striped – black, grey, a tiny bit of white and even some red here and there. She is also very fat. She wears a collar with bells around her neck. This helps do two things: One is, it warns the birds, which Mew loves to chase. And two is, it keeps her from sneaking up on you. She's very good at sneaking around. Sometimes she hides under our beds and when we walk by she jumps out. That's just her way of playing. Neither my mother nor my father is crazy about Mew and her games.

When I got to my room I closed the door with my foot and put Mew down on my bed. I flopped next to her and she stretched out. She likes me to scratch her belly. I ate my cookies and let Mew lick up the crumbs. She has never put out her claws at me. And she doesn't rip up the furniture like other cats do. It's a good thing too, because if she did we wouldn't be able to keep her.

Some people might think Mew is a dumb name for a cat. But when she came to our door two years ago she was just tiny kitten. She called *mew mew mew* and I gave her a dish of milk. She's been ours ever since. At first we all tried to think up clever names for her. But while we were thinking we got used to calling her Mew. So finally we gave up and agreed that would be her name forever.

She curled up and went to sleep as I sat down at my desk. My desk is very special. It used to be a part of somebody's dining-room set. Mom bought it for five dollars and refinished it herself. She's very good at that. Now it's bright yellow and has small gold handles on every drawer. My friends think it's neat.

I opened my middle drawer and took out my Day Book. My father gets one in the mail every December and he gives it to me. It has a plain black cover with gold letters that say *Global Insurance Company*. Inside there's a half page for every day in the year. It's not really a diary because it has no lock. It's more of an appointment book, but I don't keep a record of my appointments. If I have to go to the dentist or something like that my mother marks it on her calendar. I'm not interested in writing down that stuff.

I do keep a bunch of rubber bands wrapped around my Day Book just in case anyone happens to be snooping in my desk. They are arranged in a special way that only I understand. I took off all six of them and opened to Thursday, 25 February. At the top of the page I wrote: *Fight – E.N.'s fault*.

E.N. are my mother's initials. They stand for Ellie Newman. Her real name is Eleanor but nobody ever calls her that. My real name is Karen and nobody ever calls me anything else. It's hard to make a nickname out of Karen.

I try to be very fair about my parents' fights. Tonight was definitely my mother's fault. She should have been nicer to Daddy when he came home. She knows he likes to relax with a drink before dinner. And she shouldn't have hollered when Amy spilled her milk. That can happen to anyone.

The time Mom dropped the cake on the floor was my father's fault. He started that one by saying he hates mocha icing. So that night I wrote: *Fight*

— B.N.'s fault. My father's name is Bill — well, really William, but that's beside the point.

I put my pencil in my mouth and chewed on it for a while. When I was in first grade we had a contest to see who had the fewest teeth marks on his pencils at the end of the year. I lost. Biting on a pencil helps me think better.

I flipped back through the pages of my Day Book. I always give each day a mark, like on a report card. Practically every day this month has got a C.

My last A+ day was 14 December. That was a really perfect one. First of all, Gary Owens, who is a boy in my class, chose me as his partner in a spelling bee. I hope it wasn't just because I am a good speller. And second of all, Mrs Singer acted practically human. She didn't yell once. But the best thing about that day was the snow. We usually don't get that much snow so early in the season. It started in the morning and didn't stop until dinnertime. As soon as we finished eating, my father and Jeff went outside to shovel the walk. Me and Amy were dying to go out too. Finally Mom said, 'Okay . . . if you bundle up good and promise to come inside when you get cold.'

I helped Amy get ready. She has trouble with her boots. I tied up her hood and found her a pair of mittens. Then we went out together.

When Jeff saw us he called, 'How about a snow-ball fight? Me and Amy against Karen and Dad.'

'Okay,' we called.

Daddy and I hurried around to the side of our house and I made the snowballs for him to throw. Jeff and Amy hid behind the big tree and pretty soon the snow was flying. I think Daddy and I won but it didn't matter because it was such fun. When we got tired of throwing snowballs Amy and me lay down in the snow and made angels. I was moving my arms back and forth to make really good wings. Then I looked up at the sky. There were a million stars. I wanted everything to stay just the way it was – still and beautiful.

When we got up we were both soaked and I was sure Mom would yell at us. But we ran inside and she just laughed and told us we looked like snowmen. After we got into our pyjamas Mom made us hot chocolate with little balls of whipped cream on top. As I drank it I thought, I have never felt so good. Absolutely never!

Later I went up to my room and marked my Day Book A+. I didn't have to chew on my pencil to think it over. 14 December was perfect in every way.

But things have been going downhill since then. I'll bet my father will sleep in the den tonight. He's been doing that more and more. He tells us it's because my mother sits up in bed half the night

13

watching the late show. But my mother says she can't get to sleep because Daddy snores so loud.

I marked Thursday, 25 February C−. Then I put the rubber bands back on my Day Book and went into the bathroom to brush my teeth. Maybe tomorrow will be an A+ day. I hope so.